RISQUÉ READS
THE COMPLETE SERIES

ASHLEE ROSE

Copyright 2023 Ashlee Rose
First Edition

The author has asserted their moral right under the Copyright, Designs and Patents Act, 1988, to be identified as the author of this work.

All rights reserved. No part of this publication may be reproduced, copied, stored in a retrieval system, or transmitted, in any form by or by any means, without the prior written consent of the copyright holder, nor be otherwise circulated in any form of binding or cover other than that in which it is published and without a similar condition being imposed on the subsequent purchaser.

This is a work of fiction. Names, characters, businesses, places, events and incidents are either the products of the authors imagination or used in a fictitious manner.
Any resemblance to actual persons, living or dead, or actual events is purely coincidental.

OTHER BOOKS BY ASHLEE ROSE

Standalones:

Unwanted

Promise Me

Savage Love

Tortured Hero

Something Worth Stealing

Dear Heart, You Screwed Me

Signed, Sealed, Baby

Entwined in You Series:

Something New

Something To Lose

Something Everlasting

Before Her

Without Her

Forever Her

Illicit Love Series:

The Resentment

Duet:

Love Always, Peyton

Forever Always, Knight

Way Back When Duet

Novellas:

Welcome to Rosemont

Rekindle Us

Your Dirty Little Secret

A Savage Reunion

Risqué Read Series:

Seeking Hallow

Craving Hex

Seducing Willow

Wanting Knox

All available on Amazon Kindle Unlimited

Only suitable for 18+ due to nature of the books.

SEEKING HALLOW

READERS NOTE

This is going to be a very short story, with very little back story.

Basically, in a nutshell, it's going to be a complete fuck fest reverse harem.

If you're not into that, naughty swear words, filthy mouths, dirty sex and some hot AF scenes then maybe this book isn't for you.

Happy Halloween my little screamers, I can't wait to hear who your favourite guy is.

CHAPTER ONE
HALLOW

"Happy Birthday!" Lauren chimes out as I blow out my candle on the small, buttercream cupcake. "Make a wish!"

And I do. It's the same wish that I make every year. That the boys I crave, will finally want me back. Will finally give into the temptation they fight against every single day, well, until they up and left me.

I half smile as she picks the candle out of the cupcake and holds it out for me.

"Thank you," I just about manage as I take the cake from her and fiddle with the paper cupcake wrapper, picking at it.

"Come on, it's your birthday, you're not meant to be all gloomy and shit," she skips towards me and wraps her arm around my shoulders. "Plus, what more could you want? You've got me," she scoffs.

"I know," I mutter. Truth was, I did want more. I loved Lauren with all of my heart and I am so grateful that she was my first friend when we moved to Salem. I met her in first grade, and we graduated together when we hit seniors. Before her, it had only been me and my brother really; yes, we have parents, but they work all the time. They're the definition of workaholics. We never see them. We're like passing ships in the night. Brody has recently moved to another state for work and now we can only FaceTime as his leave is limited, so Lauren and I decided we should move out. So here we are, in a little apartment on *Essex Street* above *Caramel*. My family moved here from England when they were offered to relocate for work, but now they travel most of America heading up corporate businesses. They never go into detail but me and my brother used to tell people they were spies. It was fun.

Our apartment was cosy and monochrome. It felt cold but with our pop of colour accessories, we made it feel like home and we were grateful that we had a roof over our heads; yes rent is expensive, but we get by. *Just.*

"You ready to head out?" Lauren asks as she swipes her finger through the buttercream and licks it off in a sultry manner.

"Suppose so," I smile, shrugging my shoulders up and licking my own finger of buttercream.

"It's Halloween, party central, plus we're in Salem!"

I turn and pop the cake on the kitchen worktop behind me and reach for my bag. "Do I look okay?" Lauren asks and I smile. She is wearing a black figure hugging velvet dress with thin spaghetti straps, her make-up is flawless and she has finished her eyes with winged mascara and drew a little black nose on the tip of hers along with some whiskers on her cheeks. Her dark brown hair is straight and sitting on the top is a thin black headband with cat ears attached. Her outfit is finished off with black stiletto sandals.

"You look amazing," I nod.

"As do you," she winks.

I look at myself in the floor to ceiling length mirror by

the front door and just take a second. I chose a red PVC dress that sits just under my ass. My boobs are pushed up due to the tight material. Black smokiness surrounds my feline, green eyes and my lips are blood red. Black curls cascade down my back with a small red headband sitting with devil horns. We look so tacky and slutty but we love it.

"First stop, Jed's. House party time," Lauren jigs on the spot and I roll my eyes.

"Are we not a little old? We graduated two years ago! Aren't house parties a little too young?"

"No," she shakes her head. "It's free booze. We aren't going to be getting served in any bars are we? We're still one year away from *legally* being able to drink."

"I suppose," I step closer to the mirror and wipe a bit of smudged mascara from under my eyes. I smile back at my reflection, my freckles scattered over my nose and cheeks, the green in my eyes popping against my sun kissed skin.

"Let's go," Lauren grabs my elbow and drags me towards the door, "you need a drink, birthday girl."

"I really do," I blow out, and not because I am thirsty, but to get me through the next few hours. Lauren has had a crush on Jed for as long as I can remember but it seems he doesn't feel the same way and I know that if he gives her even a slither of his time, she will leave me in a heartbeat to be with him.

CHAPTER TWO

We've been at Jed's for an hour now and Lauren is nowhere to be seen just as I predicted. I shrug the thoughts away as I sink another drink from the famous red plastic cup. What else would I do? Go home by myself. Nah, I'll stay and enjoy the free booze. I take a moment just to stare round the room, most of the girls are in skimpy, slutty outfits like me and the guys are in random masks, mostly ghost face. *How original.* I rolled my eyes.

Sipping the vodka lemonade that I just poured myself, I drum my fingers on the skin of my thigh as the music drums through me and my hips begin to sway. The alcohol is swimming through my veins taking me one step closer to my drunken bliss. I notice three guys standing over in the far corner, facing my direction. One has a ghost face mask on, one is wearing a Guy Fawkes mask and the other is wearing a phantom of the opera mask with blood splattered across it. My skin tingles as I let my eyes rake and trail over their bodies. You could see they worked out, the muscles rippling under their tees as they moved and spoke to each other.

Averting my attention from them, I make my way up the stairs to the toilets, bumping into shoulders as I pass through the crowd. Bodies are everywhere, lips are locking and I'm pretty sure someone was just getting fucked on the stairs. *Lucky bitch.*

I can't remember the last time I was fucked properly, my last sex session was awful and when he left I let my dildo fuck me how I liked it. Hard and rough. Opening random doors and being greeted by people fucking made me giggle. Finally stumbling into the toilet, I locked the door behind me and took a breather. I did what I needed to and took my time washing my hands, before I touched up my lipstick.

Clambering back down the stairs I saw Lauren sitting on Jed's lap, her arms locked around his neck as they were kissing. I smiled, *go Lauren*. She had finally got him right where she wanted him for so long, even if it was only for tonight at least she got to have her moment.

Bumping into a rock-solid body, I stilled and looked up slowly. My eyes widening when I noticed who it was.

"I'm so sorry," I whispered, when another body pressed up behind me, hands skimming around my waist. My heart raced as the masked ghost face guy in front of me didn't move. I slowly looked behind me to see the one who was holding me was the guy wearing the phantom of the opera mask covered in blood. His ice blue eyes danced with mine and something about him seemed familiar. My skin erupted in goosebumps. Another guy appeared at my side, the one wearing the Guy Fawkes mask, his fingers wrap around the back of my neck. My blood ran cold, but I wasn't afraid of them.

Ghost face lifted his mask up, his eyes falling to look at

my heaving chest that was lifting and falling fast, my eyes widening when I realised who it was.

Rune.

"Nice to see you again pretty girl," he licks his plump lips, and one by one the others take their masks off. "As you can see, Guy is the most unoriginal out of us," his lips twitch as Guy runs his hand through his unruly, messy auburn hair and his brown eyes glisten as he pins his sights on me.

Regan's hands are still on me, the warmth radiating through me as my stomach burns with a dull ache. He edges closer to me as his lips press against my ear.

"Have you missed us?" he nips the shell of my ear and I squeeze my thighs together to try and dull the ache that is throbbing through my core and intensifying by the second.

"Why would I miss you?" I ask, my voice strong even though I am melting on the inside.

"Because you used to see us all the time until your brother told us we had to stop sniffing round you. We honoured his wish, but now he is gone we thought it was the perfect time to come back," Rune smirks, stepping closer towards me. "Happy Birthday Hallow."

He remembered, they remembered.

Rune, Regan and Guy were my brother's best friends. They were inseparable growing up but as they got older, they tried to gain my attention, little did they know that they already had it. I told them where to meet me and they didn't show. I wasn't silly. I knew what they wanted, and I was willing to give it to them; you see the thing is I already had a crush on them, every single one of them and most of my fantasies were surrounding these guys.

"Why did you let Brody stop you? You never normally listen when people tell you what to do." I argue, trying to pull away from Regan but his fingers dig into my skin as he holds me there.

"Because Brody is different, you're *different*." Rune's opal eyes dance with a slither of darkness and it sparks something deep inside of me. His dark hair has ripples of caramel entwined through it. His chiselled and strong jaw clenched and I imagine he is grinding his back teeth. Running his large hand under his chin my head turns to look at Guy, his pale skin almost glistening under the lights, his dark brown eyes move from Rune and Regan as if they're having a silent conversation between themselves.

"Anyway guys, this was lovely... well I wouldn't say lovely," I smirk to myself, "but I've got to go, I need a drink." I pull Regan's hands from my body and push through them, but I haven't gotten far when I feel a hand wrap around my wrist, pulling me back towards them.

"Not so fast pretty girl, we're not letting you back out of our sights until we're finished with you. You're not a little girl anymore Hallow," Rune licks his lips, stepping towards me he wraps his fingers around the base of my throat and Regan tugs my hair, pulling my head back. "You're a full grown ass woman now, and not under the watchful eye of Brody."

"And our new plaything," Regan teases as he presses his body into the back of me.

"And we want to play," Guy's voice is low but can still be heard over the thumping music.

I swallow, my breath catching at the back of my throat.

"I thought you said you promised Brody you wouldn't come near me," I challenge as I feel Rune's grip tighten.

"That was when he was still in Salem, but he isn't here anymore princess. And if I remember rightly," Rune taps his finger on his chin, "he did ask us to *watch* over you, didn't he boys?" his eyes don't move from mine as a menacing grin spread over his lips.

"Yes he did," Guy and Regan say in unison.

"And we need to honour our word to Brody about looking after his little sister."

I smirk, wanting to play them at their own game.

"I don't need looking after, I am quite capable of looking after myself," I pull away from their grips and stand in the middle of them. "I'm not some little girl you need to worry about anymore."

"Hallow!" Lauren calls out and the three guys turn to face her and that's when I take my chance to run for it.

"Keep running Hallow, we love to chase," Rune calls out after me as I reach Lauren, I turn to face all three of them and throw them a wink as I lick my lips. Rune's eyes narrow on me as Regan gropes his cock and Guy clenches his jaw.

They wanna play? Then I can play back.

"All okay?" Lauren asks as she side eyes the guys before focusing on me.

"Yeah fine, they're Brody's mates." I wave my hand as if it's nothing and link my arm through hers.

"Brody's mates!? Wow, they've grown buff. What did they want?" She asks as we move to the kitchen, their burning eyes still pinned to my back.

"To let me know that they're watching over me."

"I see," she looks at them once more then pours us both a Cherry Sourz shot. "Jed is pissed that they gate crashed," she says as we knock the Sourz back and she pours again.

"What's he going to do about it?" I ask as we swallow them down.

"Not a lot," she shrugs, "I'm going to go and suck his dick in a little while, keep him occupied." She wiggles her brows as she pours us another shot.

"Make sure you get some back," I frown.

"Oh I will, don't you worry about that. I've heard he is an expert pussy licker," she bites her bottom lip.

"So jealous," I sigh, "I need a good pussy eating or fuck," groaning I shot the Cherry Sourz back.

"Well by the way them three hot as fuck guys are staring at you, I think you've got some options there."

I turn my body to face them, all three of them are standing where I left them. I would be lying if I said I hadn't thought about all three of them fucking me, all three of them worshipping me, but that's all they were. Fantasies. It would be wrong, *so fucking wrong*. Wrong on so many levels.

"You going to be okay if I go back and see Jed?" Lauren smiles all goofy as she looks over at him sitting on the sofa as complete fucking chaos surrounds him. He don't give a fuck. Rich parents who let him do whatever he wants.

"I'll be fine, I have my watchers..." I giggle before hugging her, "I'll meet you back at home, okay?" I reassure her.

"Okay, if you need me, you come and get me."

I nod.

"Same for you, be safe." I wiggle my brows, "and don't forget condoms!"

She winks and skips off towards Jed whose face lights up when he sees her bounding towards him. Smiling, I turn and grab the bottle of Cherry Sourz ready to pour myself another shot when Rune's hand takes the bottle from me.

"I think you've had enough, don't you?"

"No actually, I don't," I snatch it back and take a mouthful from the bottle before it's snatched from my hands and large arms wrap around my waist, throwing me over their shoulder. Guy stands waving the bottle in front of me before taking a swig and I flip him off while I get carried out the kitchen and up the stairs.

Regan kicks one of the doors open to a large, empty room. I am dropped onto a bed, and lean up on my elbows as rage courses through me.

"Do you mind?" I snap and he smirks down at me.

"No love, I don't."

I roll my eyes and look round the extravagant room. This has got to be Jed's parents' room. There is a large wooden four poster bed, my fingers run over before scrunching the silk sheets in my hands. *Fancy*. The windows are surrounded by heavy, thick patterned curtains and a window valence in the same material. Large, mahogany oak furniture surrounds the room.

My eyes flick up from the bed when I see Rune locking the door then holding a key up and winking at me before slipping the key into one of the pockets of his black cargo pants.

"Why are you locking me in?" I lick my lips, the alcohol making me brazen, "are you going to use me?"

Rune kneels on the bed, his large hand resting on my thigh as he squeezes it, causing a gasp to leave me.

"Oh, pretty girl we're going to *use* you alright," he licks his lips quickly. "Do you know how fucking long we have waited to have you to ourselves?"

Guy stands behind Rune, and Regan moves behind me to kneel on the bed and places his hands on my shoulders, squeezing my skin as he lowers himself towards me. "Let's play a game," his voice is raspy.

Rune's eyes alight with fire and Guy pulls his bottom lip with his teeth.

"Oh, yes," Rune smirks as he moves between my thighs, widens my legs and pushes my dress up round my waist. He sucks in a breath. Regan's hand trails up and grabs a handful of my hair, snapping my head back to look at him. Guy pulls his phone out, snapping a photo of me making it look so much worse than what was actually happening.

"Now baby girl, if you refuse to play our games this photo will go to your brother and he'll see what you are, what you've always hidden from him." Rune threatens me. My pulse quickens as Regan tightens the grip on my hair, pulling at my root. "You're a little slut; we know how much you wanted us you little cock tease, and now we're going to play." He kneels away and forces my legs shut. Regan lets go of my hair and pushes me to the edge of the bed.

I'm not sure if the threat is empty, or whether they would actually send the picture to my brother, but it really doesn't matter when I already know I'll play. Why do I want them to use me? Why do I want them to use me as bait?

"And what game are we going to play?"

"First," Guy smirks as he stands from the bed, "we're going to play truth or dare." I scoff a snort.

"Truth or dare?" I laugh, "isn't that for twelve-year-olds?" My eyes move between the three of them.

"Not the way we play it, love," Regan rolls his lips.

"Rune, truth?" Guy barks at him and Rune nods. "Is it true that all you could think about over the last couple of years was Hallow?" Guy smirks and Regan rubs his hands together.

Rune's opal eyes drag from Guy to me as he looks me up and down, licking his lips as if waiting to devour me. "If you mean thinking about sinking my cock into her pussy and fucking her until she physically cannot take any more, then yeah, I couldn't stop thinking about her."

The ache grows between my legs, and I press my thighs together to try and give myself some relief.

"Are you getting turned on Hallow? Are you getting wet at the thought of me fucking you until you're sore?" Rune moves forward, wrapping his fingers round the base of my throat and smiles down at me, "tell me pretty girl, what can I do to you?"

My wide, big, green eyes settle on his and I grin.

"I want you to play truth or dare."

He leans down and clasps my cheeks with his fingers, smirking before he takes my bottom lip between his teeth, "Good girl. You don't know what you've just asked for," his gruff voice vibrates through me and my core tightens at the thought. I know I am playing with fire, but it's too late.

CHAPTER THREE
RUNE

My inner thoughts are going wild. *We finally have her. Is she going to let us actually have her? All the things I have thought about doing to her, I get to relive each and every one of my fantasies alongside the boys. My best mates.*

"I want you to play truth or dare," her voice is soft but her eyes are ablaze with want.

I lean down, our faces close to each other as I grab her cheeks with my hand, digging my fingers into the soft flesh. I bite out, pulling on her bottom lip and tug. "Good girl. You don't know what you've just asked for," my voice is low and gruff. Dropping her face, I push her back on the bed and take a moment to let my thoughts settle.

Regan and Guy are by my side, both of their silent questions being thrown at me. Closing my eyes, I inhale deeply before letting them open and pinning them on her and only her. I nod my head back towards the door and turn, the boys following me.

"I have one request," my voice is low so she can't hear me.

"Yeah?" Guy asks.

"I'm the first one to fuck her pussy," I groan, my cock hard as I palm it through my cargos.

"Deal," Regan and Guy nod.

"Let's fucking play, boys," we spin and see her still sitting on the comforter, her long legs are crossed and one of her black stiletto heels rests on the floor. The shoes need to stay. Her tight as fuck PVC dress leaves nothing to the imagination. We can see every curve of her body.

Stepping towards her, her eyes volley between the three of us and she smirks.

"Okay, so how is this going to work?" she asks, pushing her arms behind her and falling back so she is putting her weight on her hands.

"Like truth or dare," Guy sniggers and I roll my eyes, swatting him. *Dick.* "Well, we will take it in turns... Rune, want to start?"

"Truth or dare, pretty girl?" I lick my lips.

"Truth," she pouts, her eyes locking with mine.

"Is it true that you have fantasised about all three of us doing things to you?" Regan asks, stepping up behind me and glowering down at her on the bed.

"Yes," her voice is barely audible, "whenever I have touched myself the focal thinking point is you three."

"Fuck," Regan sucks air in through the small gap in his front teeth causing a whistle.

"Guy," her timid voice fills the room as her eyes pin to Guy, "truth or dare?" her tongue darts out and wets her bottom lip.

"Dare," his eyes hood as he glares down at her. She sits up slowly, twirling her finger in the curl of her hair before standing up and stepping towards him, placing her hand on Guy's chest and hovering her lips just over his.

"I want you to kiss Regan," her head slowly turns to

look at Regan and she bites her bottom lip before placing her lips at Guy's ear, "it would *really* turn me on."

She's a little minx. She knows what she is doing. I smirk, letting my head drop as I scoff.

"Not a problem princess," Guy steps forward, gently pushing her out the way as he clasps Regan's face and locks lips with him. My brows lift, I'm surprised, I thought Regan would have pushed away but it just shows how needy we are for her, we would do *anything*.

Guy breaks away and shrugs his shoulders up, "Piece of piss," he licks his lips, "now it's your turn."

"Dare." She says all bold.

"Get on your fucking knees," I growl, and she does. Regan drops down beside her and pulls her dress up roughly round her waist, palming her bare ass cheek as his lips press to her neck licking and sucking on her skin.

I stand in front of her, running my thumb over her pouty bottom lip then smudge her red lipstick over her cheek, "I'm going to ruin your pretty fucking make-up."

Unbuttoning my cargos, I slip them down slightly and fist my cock in my boxers, her greedy hands reach up and pull my boxers down. Her eyes widen in delight as she takes me in, her eyes falling to my cock before they flick up to meet mine.

"I dare you to show me how well you suck my cock, show me how you have fantasised about sucking me."

The fucking smile that crosses her lips is enough to make me explode over her face. Licking her lips, she edges closer and purses her lips round my tip, swallowing me down.

"Fuck," I grit, my hips thrusting forward so I hit the back of her throat. Regan continues rubbing and kneading her ass, his fingers teasing and slipping inside her lace panties. Guy stands behind her, his eyes low as he watches me fuck her mouth, his hands pulling his cock from his trousers as he begins to pump himself.

Reaching forward, I grab a fistful of her hair and push her head back and forth.

"Look how fucking pretty you look with your mouth full of my cock," I groan, thrusting my hips forward, making her choke.

Regan's lips trace along her jaw line before he licks her tears away. Her lipstick is smudging, saliva hangs at the corners of her mouth as I continue to fill her.

"You're going to swallow my cum, and then I'm going to let the boys play with you and use you like the little slut I know you are," I tighten my grip on her hair as Regan smirks, his eyes lifting from her to me. Guy groans as his pumps become slow and lazy.

"Hold off Guy, don't waste your cum on your hand," I snap. Pulling my cock out to the tip, I let it sit on her plump lips. Her eyes pin to mine, smudged in mascara and glistening with fresh, unshed tears. Slamming my hips forward hard and fast I feel her retch, but she holds me at the back of her throat before I fuck her mouth. Regan is getting impatient, he is biting and nipping along her shoulder, his fingers digging into her exposed skin. Guy steps back, waiting his turn.

Her small hand reaches up and wraps around the base of my cock as she takes control, sucking and licking the head of my cock before taking me to the back of her throat. I let my head fall back as pleasure ripples through me. Something inside me snaps and I go savage, feral as I pull her hand away from me. Both my hands are in her hair as I tug at her root and fuck her mouth hard and fast. She hollows her cheeks and swallows me down as I hit the back of her throat, her eyes stream as hot tears roll down her cheeks but I'm not stopping until I spurt my cum down the back of her throat. Guy steps forward, grabbing her curls and holding them away from her face as I continue fucking her mouth. His thumb pad swipes at the saliva that's escaped her lips before he pops his thumb into his mouth and sucks it. She stifles a moan round my cock and I see Regan's hand grabbing her thigh while the other kneads her full breast. I drop my hands from her hair.

"Fuck," I roar, my cock twitching and bobbing. "Fucking look at me, open your eyes," I growl, and she does as I ask.

"So fucking obedient," her tongue flattens under my throbbing cock and her eyes stay glued to mine as I spurt my cum onto her tongue and just before I am finished, I rub my thumb over my sensitive tip then drag it across from the corner of her mouth so my cum glistens on her cheek.

I smile at her, my heart thumping in my chest, the blood pumping to my aching cock. Grabbing her chin, I tilt her head back, "Such a good girl."

Regan sucks her neck which causes her head to fall back against his chest.

"Get her on the bed," I order and Regan moves her.

"Game time baby," Regan says as he steps back, "it's game time."

CHAPTER FOUR
HALLOW

My throat feels hoarse, but I loved it. Every single minute of him throat fucking me. His thick, large cock felt good in my mouth, and I want Regan and Guy to do it now. I roll my lips, licking my lips as my nipples harden at the thought.

Regan and Guy kneel on the bed, one either side of me while Rune stands at the end of the bed, his eyes penetrating mine. The pull is there, the burn evident in my stomach from just his look. I clench my throbbing pussy as Regan pushes my legs wide for them all to see.

"You all wet you little slut?" Rune teases as he leans down, resting his hands on the end of the bed. "Did you enjoy me throat fucking you? I knew you would." Rune nods to Regan who grabs the thin material of my lace panties and tugs them down my legs where Rune takes over and slips them over my heels. He brings them to his nose and inhales deeply before throwing them to Guy who literally buries his nose deep inside before tossing them over to Regan who does the same. My insides quiver.

Guy groans, his hand slipping between my legs as he grips my inner thigh, his fingers brushing ever so softly against my sex. My eyes flutter shut as my skin tingles and my breath catches. Regan lowers his lips over mine, dipping his tongue between my cushioned lips, teasing me when I all I want is for him to desperately kiss me.

Guy's fingers edge closer to my pussy, pulling my lips slightly before letting his fingers trail on my inner thigh.

"Truth or dare, pretty girl?" Regan whispers against my lips, then covering my mouth with his. His warm tongue is laced with mint and Cherry Sourz as he explores my mouth, my tongue eagerly stroking and dancing with his. Our kiss is hot, wet and messy.

"Truth," I gasp as Guy slaps my clit, my pussy throbbing. My legs quiver but Guy pushes both of them down while Regan holds my cheeks within his grasp, teasing my mouth with his tongue.

"She's got such a pretty cunt," Guy groans. "Has anyone fucked your ass before?" Guy's voice is low as he trails is finger down my slit and presses the tip of his finger at my tight hole.

My hips buck forward, writhing under their tight grip. I hear the sound of a phone camera snapping and I moan.

"Answer the question, *Bella*," Rune curls his tongue at the nickname.

"No," I gasp, my chest heaving up and down.

"Let me have her ass, Rune," Regan practically begs against my lips as his teeth graze down along my jaw.

Two thick fingers push inside me, hard and fast and I cry out.

"Fuck, you need to feel her pussy, so fucking tight," Guy growls as he fucks me relentlessly with his fingers. Regan drops my cheeks from his tight grip and I want to rub the ache out but before I even get the chance Regan wraps one of his hands round both of my wrists and pins them above my head, he winks before letting his eyes fall between my legs.

Guy pulls his fingers to the tip, pulling his cock out with his spare hand he rubs himself in slow, torturous pumps.

Regan adjusts my wrists so he retrains both with one of his hands before he licks his lips as his now free finger lines up above Guy's slick ones and pushes inside me at the same time. Regan's eyes roll in the back of his head as he sinks his teeth into his bottom lip.

I clench my pussy, the dull ache intensifying with every pump of their fingers. My hazy eyes find Rune, his jaw is clenched, his eyes dark and hooded as he watches his friends finger fuck me.

My moans fill the room, my hips bucking as I grind down on their fingers. My orgasm is teetering, I am close to free falling, my body weightless as I wait to crash into my own pleasure pool.

"Don't let her come," Rune snaps, "I want her to come on my cock and only on my cock."

Tears roll down my cheeks at the intensity of feeling so full, but I know this is nothing to how I will feel later this evening.

Regan and Guy pull their fingers out to the tip, holding it there as my body trembles. I am trying my hardest to not give in to the orgasm that is burning through me, my pussy aches with release and all I want to do is let it go.

"Let her sit up," Regan orders Guy as he pulls his finger from me but Guy doesn't withdraw, I lift myself on shaky arms and shuffle my bum back towards the headboard and as I move, Guy curls his fingers and rubs the spot that has been begging to be touched, making me moan loudly.

"Don't fucking come," Rune scolds, moving round the bed and leaning over me, "do you understand, pretty girl?"

he smirks before his fingers slap my clit. My head falls back as my legs tremble.

Regan grabs my cheeks, turning me to face him as he pulls his cock from his pants, pressing the tip at my lips.

"Open wide," he winks as his cock fills my mouth. My eyes flutter shut as Guy's fingers still pump slowly inside of me, pulling to the tip, edging me as my orgasm builds.

My jaw aches, but I suck on his cock as he slams his hips forward, hitting the back of my throat. My eyes well as he continues.

"Look at me while I fuck your mouth, baby girl," and I do as he asks, a tear escaping but he swipes it away with his thumb pad. Guy pulls his fingers from me and shoves them past Rune's lips and he hums.

"You get first taste, bro," he groans as he goes back to stroking himself. Rune dives forward, kneeling between my legs and pressing my thighs apart and flat to the bed.

"Suck my cock you little slut," Regan slaps my cheek, his hands in my hair as he fucks my face. I pull my hand from his grip and tighten it around his cock, licking and sucking him as I take control. My eyes move to Guy who is hovering over my stomach jerking himself off. I let them trail to Rune who is frozen, his fingers digging into the skin of my thigh.

"That's it, fucking swallow it," Regan spits, as I slide his cock down the back of my throat as he spurts his hot cum. Pulling him out, I let the tip of his cock sit on my lips as I lick him clean. He falls back, his fingers wrapped around his cock as he comes down from his orgasm.

My eyes move back to Rune, the darkness enticing me in. I smirk at him, my hands trailing to my breasts as I pinch my nipples through the tight PVC material.

"Your cunt is glistening," he rasps, pressing down on my thighs harder as he leans over, bending down and spits on my clit before flattening his tongue and licking me from my clit to my opening, pressing his tongue inside of me.

"Oh fuck," I cry, watching him between my legs. He repeats once more then swirls his tongue over my clit.

Guy's hand darts out, wrapping round the base of my throat as he moves up the bed and pushes his thick cock into my mouth.

"My turn," he grins down at me.

"You taste like fucking heaven," Rune murmurs against my skin as his lips trail along the inside of my thigh, three of his thick fingers pushing into me.

I moan around Guy's cock, the saltiness already coating my tongue, he's already close. Hollowing my cheeks, I suck his cock hard, taking him down the back of my throat and holding him there, his cock twitches and bobs as he comes and I swallow every drop of him. He pulls out then lowers his lips to mine as his tongue swirls with mine. Panting, I break the kiss and Guy winks before moving off the bed. I take a moment, just watching him before my attention is back on Rune.

"Truth or dare, Rune?" Guy licks his lips, his hands crossed in front of him as Regan steps up beside him.

Rune kneels up, holding his hand out for me to take. My hand trembles, but not through fear; no, but through over stimulation. My nerve endings are shot, my insides like a ticking time bomb ready to explode at any moment, one slip of the finger and I'm gone. Brushing a loose curl behind my ear, his hands skim down the side of my body and tug my dress down to cover my little modesty.

"Dare," his tongue swipes across his bottom lip, his eyes steady with Regan's who raises his eyebrows then turns his head slowly towards Guy. He cocks his head to the side before letting it roll forward and his eyes meeting Rune's.

My heart thumps, my adrenaline spikes as I keep still on the bed.

"Pretty girl," the nickname sounds heavenly on his tongue, and my eyes haze, my heart races. Chewing the inside of my mouth, I twist my lips as my doe eyes gaze at him.

"I dare you to run," his lips turn slowly at the corners into a delicious smirk.

"Run?" I stammer as my eyes trail round the room at all three of them.

"Run," Guy nods. I don't move, unsure if they're being serious or not.

"Think of it like a game of kiss chase, you run away and if we find you, well..." Rune pulls his bottom lip between his teeth and sucks it in. I swallow.

"Run dollface," Guy leans across the bed, his hands lost in the comforter and I shift, sliding off the bed. As soon as my feet hit the floor, Rune is behind me, fingers wrapped round the base of my neck, his spare hand skimming under my dress as he rubs my clit through my soaked panties. His breath is on the back of my neck making my hairs stand on end, his lips trailing round to the shell of my ear as he licks slowly. Regan walks towards the door, unlocking it and standing back. Reality hits me in the face, my stomach coiling when Rune's lips hover over my ear.

"Run," he whispers.

And I do.

I bolt. Fear, lust, adrenaline course through my veins, my blood thumping and rushing as my heart rate spikes and all I can do is run.

CHAPTER FIVE

Running down the stairs, missing steps as I go, I look behind me and breathe out a quick sigh of relief that they're not following. *Yeah Yeah – Bodyrox* blasts through the house, the music pumping through me making everything vibrate. Kicking my heels off, I leave them and push through the crowds that seem to have doubled since I have been upstairs. As I pass the lounge I try to look for Lauren but I can't see her. I internally cuss before I run out the back door and onto the deck, the chill in the air covering me in goosebumps but I draw in a deep breath and let the cold air fill my lungs, gasping as I do. I push through, running onto the back lawn past stoners and smokers and slip into the woods with only myself and the shadows.

It's like a fucked up game of cat and mouse, but either way it has the same outcome. We both get devoured.

Stopping, I give myself a minute to catch my breath. I want to be caught, my pussy is aching with need for release, and I know they'll make sure I get it but they want to play. They want to tease and break me. Use me like the little whore they know I am.

But only for them.

How I've been fucked is nothing in comparison to what these boys are going to do to me. They will fill every hole, filling me to the hilt for my own pleasure. The growing ache deepens, the slow burn growing more torturous as my thoughts intensify. Leaning against a tree, the mist begins to fall and hazes what's in front of me. Fear coats me but I don't move. Letting my head fall back, I close my eyes for a moment.

What must I look like? Bare foot, smudged red lipstick and blackened eyes.

How long do I stay here for before I head back? Suddenly it feels a lot cooler and a shiver blankets me. I step forward, but the sound of a twig snapping makes me still.

"We told you to run, baby," Regan's voice echoes. I smirk, licking the corner of my mouth.

"I did run," I call out to the mist, not knowing what direction they're coming from.

"Well you didn't run very far, you were easy to track," Guy tsks, I turn behind me but I don't see him.

"Look at you, standing there like *a beautiful fucking mess*," Rune's voice slips through the cool, dark evening. "A mess we made, but once we're finished with you..." he stops, *"you're going to be a beautiful disaster."*

That's when I see them.

Striding towards me with their masks on, and I quiver. I don't know what it is with them wearing those masks, but it lights something deep, *deep* inside of me and all I can think about is when they eventually fuck me, I want them wearing the masks.

CHAPTER SIX
REGAN

Breaking through the mist we finally lay eyes on her. She is still, quiet. She steps forward just as we move towards her. The twig breaking makes her think twice.

She is a sight for sore eyes, and I can't wait to sink my cock inside of her to see what else we can do to her.

"We told you to run, baby," my voice is loud, causing an echo. My cock twitches as she smirks, licking the corner of her mouth and in that moment I want to suck on her tongue.

"I did run," She calls out to the misted darkness of the woods, her eyes constantly darting around to work out where the sound is coming from.

"Well you didn't run very far, you were easy to track," Guy tsks. She spins round and Guy lets out a low, quiet rumble. We take another slow, small step towards her as she spins back round.

"Look at you, standing there like *a beautiful fucking mess*. A mess we made, but once we're finished with you..." Rune pauses, no doubt for dramatic effect, *"you're going to be a beautiful disaster."*

I groan, hard and feeling too constricted against my pants.

"Let me have her, fuck, I need her," I beg to Rune as her eyes take us all in, her chest heaving.

"Do your worst," Rune's voice is quiet, "but I mean it Regan, her fucking pussy is mine." He warns and I fucking hear him loud and clear. Rune and Guy stay back as I break towards her, pushing her against the tree, pinning her there with my fingers wrapped around her throat.

My eyes fall to her heaving chest and I groan. Tightening my grip, I edge towards her and lick from her jaw to her ear and suck on her lobe.

"Regan," she pants.

"Yes baby," I nip, letting go of her throat and skimming my hands down the side of her body. Gripping under her perfect ass, I squeeze and pick her up, smiling as she wraps her legs round my waist. I push my hips into her as a gasp leaves her lips. "You feel that, sweetheart? That's all for you..." I lick my bottom lip and pull it between my teeth. "The only problem is, I promised Rune I wouldn't fuck your cunt, I mean, I will... but he gets it first." I pant, her wet, covered pussy grinding over me. "You keep doing that princess, I'm going to come in my boxers and no one wants that."

She grins, her arms tightening around my neck as she circles her hips slowly.

"Stop it," I groan.

She doesn't.

"Stop being a *tease*," I drawl out the last word.

"I need you," her voice is desperate and needy and it drives me fucking insane. I growl, letting my hands roam up, I grip the top of her cheap PVC dress and rip it in a blind rage as testosterone erupts through me.

She gasps as I rip it in two and discard the shards of material to the floor.

"So much better," I smile, my lips on her neck as I suck and nip along her vein that beats under her skin. Sinking my teeth in a little harder my large hand kneads her full breast, pulling and rolling her hardened nipple between my fingers. Her head falls forward and I tug it back, "You'll fucking look at me, your eyes stay *on me*." I grit, my jaw tics.

Pressing my hips forward, I pin her to the tree. "Do you understand?" my voice is low as her eyes glisten.

"Yes," she whispers.

"There's a good girl," I praise, placing a soft kiss on her forehead and let her have her legs back. Trailing wet and hot kisses along her collar bone, I continue over her bare tits, licking and sucking, marking her skin. I smirk against her skin as I look up at her through my lashes. Gliding my lips down her sternum, slowly trailing them across her navel before stopping above her panty line. An animalistic primal feeling takes over, pressing my nose into her soaked cunt through the thin material I inhale deeply.

"Shit." I fall back onto my knees and take a second to look at the beauty that stands before me.

A growl rumbles deep in my throat, I tear her laced panties and let them disintegrate in my hands.

"Fuck's sake," I hear Rune curse and I laugh as I dive in, parting her pussy lips with my fingers and suck on her clit.

Fuck me. She tastes indescribable. Sweet and salty but also so fucking addicting.

She moans as I swirl my tongue over her clit and sink it into her soaked opening.

"Regan," she pants, her fingers locking in my hair as she tugs hard, silently begging me to make her come.

My fingers are still in place, pulling her apart resisting

the urge to split her in two with my thick and throbbing cock. Turning my head slightly, I see Guy and Rune appear, their eyes dark and hazy as they watch her.

Guy moves to his knees, his callous and rough fingers gliding up and down her thigh before his fingertips graze through her slit and tease at her opening. Her hips buck forward, gliding on my tongue as he pushes three fingers inside of her.

He grins, looking at her glistening cunt. "Look how fucking pretty she looks stretched around me," he groans as he fucks her with his fingers hard and fast.

Rune's lips graze along her jaw line, his hand wrapping around her throat to hold her in place to stop her squirming.

"Stop moving, little one," he whispers against the shell of her ear but loud enough for me and Guy to hear. His lips trail down the side of her face, nipping at her jaw as he sucks on her neck.

"Guy, fuck, taste her," I groan as I watch him fuck her with his fingers and I move back, his tongue swiping through her folds and he moans, burying his face. I lift her legs, placing them over Guy's shoulders as he eats her as if she is his last meal. Her wails and moans echo round the woods as Rune's expert fingers roll her nipples between his fingers before locking his lips around them, sucking and flicking his tongue. Rising up onto my feet, I push my pants down, and fist myself and begin pumping my cock slow and hard. Stepping forward, I grab Guy's auburn hair, tugging his head back as I smash my lips into his, my tongue plunging past his lips, desperate to taste her on his tongue.

Pulling away from Guy, I see Rune's fingers skim down her sheen covered skin as he rubs her swollen clit, Guy growls as he turns his attention to her pussy, teasing her with his fingers.

"I need more," I groan like an addict, itching and constantly looking for their next hit. I am so close to exploding but I need to hold off. Standing on the other side of Hallow, I run my fingers under her ass cheeks as Guy places her legs back over his shoulders and I dip my fingers into her soaked cunt, plunging them into her slowly while Rune works her clit, his lips pressed to her exposed skin on her neck.

"Oh shit," she cries as Rune spreads her pussy lips open, letting Guy devour her while I fuck her with my fingers.

"What's the matter pretty girl?" Rune smirks against her neck as his free hand grabs and squeezes her tit in his large hand.

"I'm so close," she pants, her eyes falling down as she watches Guy eat her.

"How close?" my lips press against the back of her thigh, baring my teeth and grazing them against her flesh as I continue slow pumps of my fingers, curling and rubbing her spot. She is fucking soaked.

"Close," she trembles as Rune takes her weight, her back scratched and marked from the bark as Guy presses her harder into it.

Guy spreads her legs, parting her further as he enjoys every bit of her.

"Well, love..." I grin, pulling my fingers out and using her arousal as lube as I rub the tips of my fingers over her tight, puckered ass.

"You're about to come so fucking hard," I promise as I press two fingers inside of her ass, biting down on her skin as I fuck her ass with my fingers slowly. "I am just stretching you for my cock," I tease as Guy sucks on her clit, moaning as he does. Rune sinks his teeth into her neck as he works her nipples. I smile as her whole body convulses, trembling and shaking as she cries out into the darkness. Guy's mouth widens as he licks and sucks every drop of her. He falls back, smiling as her cum glistens on his lips and nose. He fucking ate her deep.

Her whole-body slumps as Guy places her legs down and Rune holds her up.

Pulling my fingers out, I stand and pull her out of Rune's grip, my kisses pressing over the blood on her neck from where Rune took it a little too far on his biting.

"I knew you would enjoy my fingers in your ass, wait till it's my dick ripping through and fucking you so hard you'll be sobbing," I threaten, my teeth grazing down across her collar bone. Guy pulls his tee over his head and dresses her.

"Better find your energy pretty girl, we're ready for the next game," Rune smiles as she pants.

"Hide and seek," Guy rubs his hands together, "and once we have found you, we're going to fuck and fill every part of you."

CHAPTER SEVEN
HALLOW

I RUN.

I run for my life until I reach a small cabin at the back of the woods. This is like every horror movie, you never run further into the woods, you run out of the woods. Tugging on the door, it's locked and my heart jack-hammers in my chest.

"No, no, no," I cry out, pulling it harder.

"Hello love," Guy steps round the corner, dangling a key in front of me. My eyes widen.

"Was you hoping to hide in here little one?" He teases, closing the gap between us.

"Seemed that way," my voice is strong as I turn to face him.

"That's a shame," he shrugs, squeezing my ass cheek as he moves next to me to open the cabin door.

He looks at me over his shoulder, smirking at me, "Coming?"

I nod, rubbing my lips as I step over the threshold. The musky smell of the wood fills my nostrils, but somehow it smells like home. I knot my fingers as I stand there in just

Guy's tee, goosebumps smother me suddenly. I feel cold, damp.

"Come and have a shower, baby. It'll warm you up," Guy chucks the keys on the worktop of the spacious cabin.

"Where are Rune and Regan?" I ask, turning to look at the darkness of the woods through the windows.

"They're coming, just had to stop off quickly," he licks his lips as he holds his hand out for me to take, which I do.

"So you live here?" I ask as I take in my surroundings.

"We do live here, yeah," he gives me a half lopsided smile.

"It seems peaceful," I whisper as I step into the warm bathroom. He lets go of my hand and reaches over to turn the shower on. The pipes bang through the cabin. Turning, he closes the gap between us and tugs at the hem of my tee, smirking.

"Let's get this off you, shall we?" Winking, he slowly pulls it over my head and tosses it in the wash basket that is sat in the corner of the room. His hands cup my face, the pads of his thumb swiping across my lips.

"You're trembling," he whispers and I see a flash of worry fill his eyes, "you okay?"

I nod, sinking my teeth into my bottom lip.

"Just a little cold."

He leads me to the shower then lets go of my hand. "Warm up, I'll be in the kitchen when you're done," he smiles sweetly at me. My heart skips.

"You're leaving?"

"Yeah," he rolls his lips, "because if I stay, I'll have no self-control. Rune gets you before any of us. Pecking order and all that," he smirks, his hand rubbing the top of his mop of auburn hair.

"What do you get?" I whisper as I stand tall.

"The leftovers," he licks his lips slowly and closes the door.

My heart swells before it shatters, crashing through my chest in an instant.

I have always loved these three men, and now I have finally got a taste of what it could be like for them to love me back, I am terrified of having to walk away.

Wiping the steam off the mirror in the bathroom, I look at the girl looking back at me. My eyes are bright and full of lust, my dark hair is damp and sitting over my shoulder and I smile. My eyes trail down across my collar bone before they widen, turning when I see the love bites that Rune has marked my skin with and suddenly, I am hot and bothered and panting to have him mark me even more.

Padding out to the kitchen in the fresh t-shirt that Guy left on the towel warmer, I pull out a seat at the breakfast bar.

"Better?" he asks.

"Better," I nod, even though the feeling of nausea rips through me at my earlier thoughts. Bringing the tee to my nose I inhale and smell Rune's scent all over it.

My eyes dart up as Regan and Rune walk through the door.

"You found her then?" Rune licks his lips.

"Yup, ran straight to the cabin in the woods..." Guy smirks.

Regan strides towards me, his cold fingers digging into my cheeks as he grips my face.

"Silly, naive little girl. Never *ever* run into the woods. Don't you remember the story about the big bad wolf?" he snarls.

I lick my lips.

"Difference is, there are three of us here, not just one," his voice is a low, guttural growl. The delicious burn begins to swirl and grow deep in my lower belly and I gasp as Regan's lips smash into mine, his tongue sweeping across my bottom lip before dipping it inside my mouth.

"Leave her," Rune snaps and Regan drops my face, stepping back and turning to face Rune.

"Go get cleaned up," he barks at Regan, "Guy, give us a minute or two..." he nods towards his friend before Guy disappears down the hallway. Regan follows on his heels and slams the bathroom door.

"You okay?" Rune asks, and it's the first time I've heard kindness in his tone.

"Yeah," I pick the skin round my nails.

"Sure?"

I nod.

"Because what we're about to do to you... all of us..." he licks his lips quickly, letting his opal eyes fall before they penetrate through me, "there's no going back."

My insides quiver and my pussy pulses at the thought.

"I know," I whisper, my gaze on him, "I want it. All of it..." I trail off, rubbing my lips, "all of you."

His head tips back, his Adam's apple bobs in his throat before his eyes find mine again, dark and hooded. I don't have a moment to catch my breath before he wraps his arms around my waist and throws me over his shoulder, my tee rising up as his large hand kneads my bare ass. Turning his head, he sinks his teeth hard into my skin and kicks the bedroom door shut behind him. Dropping me to the bed, his fingers dig into the skin on my thighs, dragging me to the edge of the bed where he kneels.

"I am going to eat you, then I am going to fuck your tight little cunt before the boys are allowed in to play."

His large hands skim under my grey tee, pushing it up to expose my bare skin, his fingers tracing lightly against my hot skin.

"Rune," I whisper, his lips kissing my thighs, as his hands pin my waist to the bed so I can't move.

"Yes, pretty girl."

"Eat me, devour me like you've promised," leaning up on my elbows I gaze at him between my legs, "I *need* you."

Rune pushes my legs apart, spitting on my pussy. Not that I need the extra lube, I am soaked already.

"Play with yourself you little slut, show me how you get yourself off when you think of me, of *us*."

Lifting one of my elbows, I let my fingers glide towards my pussy. Softly rubbing my clit, in large, slow circles. My eyes flutter shut, my breath shuddering.

"Eyes on me, don't you dare fucking move them off me."

Letting them open slowly, heaviness fills my eyes as lust overtakes them.

"Such a pretty little cunt," he groans, teasing three fingers at my opening as he stretches me. "Just warming you up for what you have to come," I clench, tightening around his fingers as my fingers stay rubbing my clit softly.

"What do you do when you're at home? When we invade your thoughts..." he licks his lips, his eyes falling from mine and watches me touch myself.

I stay mute.

"Tell me," he growls.

"I use my dildo, fuck myself so hard that my whole-body aches once I come," I moan, "but it's just not enough, I need so much more," my fingers rub faster, his fingers begin to fuck me.

"Well, pretty girl, you're going to get fucked raw."

I hum, slipping my fingers down my folds and quiver when I feel his fingers are deep inside of me.

"Fuck," my voice shakes as I try to hold off my impending orgasm. Moving my fingers back to my swollen clit, I rub faster, harder.

"That's it baby, show me how you make yourself come," he groans, his lips pressing on the inside of my thighs, my hips bucking forward as I grind over his fingers as I try to take him deeper.

"Stop being a greedy little slut," his voice is tight and raspy.

"I can't help it," I beg, my voice a slight whine, "I need more."

"I know baby, and I am going to give it..." he trails off, "as soon as you come over my fingers."

He rips my hand from my pussy and covers my pussy with his mouth. Sucking and flicking his tongue over my clit, grinding my hips over his fingers.

His tongue swirls slowly, before he sucks hard on my swollen clit and I come so. Fucking. Hard.

My head falls back, my legs tremble and I tighten around his fingers.

"You're such a good girl," he groans, slipping his fingers out and kneeling between my legs. He leans over me, his breath shaky as he pushes his three fingers past my lips.

"Suck them fucking clean," he orders and I do, like a needy fucking girl who wants to do anything to please him.

"I want you to fuck me with your mask on," I cry out as he slaps my clit, falling back on his knees.

"Oh, pretty girl..." He licks his lips, rubbing his chin as his thumb presses across his bottom lip, "I am going to fucking ruin you."

CHAPTER EIGHT
RUNE

She's on all fucking fours, her legs spread as I look at her tight, glistening cunt. I am waiting for the guys to come back in, but they're taking forever. I lay down under her and grab her hips as I lower her pussy onto my lips, flicking my tongue over her clit. She falls forward, her pert little tits bouncing as I rock her hips back and forth over my mouth. The bedroom door closes and I feel the bed dip. Guy kneels over me, pushing four fingers into her tight cunt and Regan stays at her head, pushing his thumb into her mouth while rubbing himself off.

"She's so fucking wet," Guy hisses, his thumb pressing across her ass which causes her to shudder.

"I need more," she moans round Regan's thumb and his eyes lock on Guy's. They move back, giving me a minute to eat her pussy. Pushing her away, but keeping her on all fours I sit on my knees. Slipping my ghost face mask on, her sparkling green eyes find me as she looks over her shoulder and smirks. Edging closer to her, I rub the tip of my swollen cock through her soaked folds, nudging my head at her opening to tease her. I give her a moment, her mewls filling the room as I push my hips forward as I edge into her, trying to fill her to the fucking hilt as I let her pussy adjust.

"Oh, God, fuck," she cries, rocking her hips back and forth, "you're too big," she chokes. "You're not going to fit," she sobs, clenching.

"I'm no God pretty girl," I pull out slightly, then edging in a little deeper "I'm the fucking devil," I groan, my head tipping back as I slip out right to my tip, then pushing into her once more, "and I'll fucking make it fit," my cock filling her deep. "Your pussy looks so fucking good full of my cock." My hands tightening around her small waist, lifting her ass in the air as I slip to the tip and slam back in again.

"Rune," she chokes as I begin to fuck her relentlessly, I lean across her back and grab a handful of her hair, tugging her back so she is on my lap and I smile beneath the mask knowing that they have their phones in their hands.

"Take the fucking photo," I grit as I hold off, her legs spread across my toned, thick thighs and I am adamant I am about to split her in fucking two.

Snap.

"Rune," I can hear the panic in her voice.

"Baby, the shit we're going to be doing to you... we need to let you know that we aren't going to be stopping at anything."

Holding onto her hips, I thrust up into her, the sound of our skin slapping as I fuck her cunt hard and fast, pounding into her.

"Boys, her fucking pussy is to die for," I clench my jaw as Guy climbs on the bed, his fingers rubbing over her clit, his lips pressing to hers as he kisses her. His large hand moves to the back of her head, holding her in place as I rock into her. His fingers brush against my balls, making me flinch as he presses two fingers inside of her and she gasps, but her pussy stretches taking us both.

"I'm telling you, a little bit of practice and we could both fuck her pussy," Guy's voice is thick as he swallows and my cock bobs at the thought.

"Pull out of her," I grit and Guy does, moving back.

"Tie her arms behind her back," Regan orders and Guy reaches for black ribbon, tying it tight around her wrists and binding her arms behind her back.

I push her forward so her ass is in the air and I spank her hard.

"Such an obedient little slut," I spank her again, this time, my hand print marks her.

"I am going to fuck you hard, and once I am done, I am going to move you on top of me, then I'll let Regan fuck your ass at the same time, do you understand?" I lean down next to her, my lips by her ear and her watery eyes pin to mine as she nods.

"Good girl."

Kneeling behind her, I slip back in with ease and fuck her raw.

Guy sits in front of her, his eyes locking with mine as he smirks, his hard cock in his hand and I nod. I watch as he grabs a fistful of her hair, and pushes her lips down on his dick, choking her and I feel every muscle contract.

"What a sight, greedy girl," I groan as I fuck her pussy until I can't ride her anymore, I pull out and slap her ass cheek hard. I roll on my back, reaching across I lift her up, pulling her over to slam her down onto my dick. Guy groans at the loss of her hot mouth, but he'll have to wait his turn.

"Lean over me, let Regan see that pretty little ass."

Her hips move back and forth, rocking over my cock and I swear I am about to bust because her pussy feels too good.

Regan growls, his fingers slipping in over my cock and fucking her to coat his fingers in her arousal before rubbing them over her ass.

I can see the red haze in his eyes, he is too far gone to be soft.

"Hold on baby," I reassure her, my fingers digging into her hips as Regan thrusts his hips and fills her ass in one swift move, not giving her a chance. He stills as she cries out, her pussy clenching as she adjusts to being filled by both of us.

"Oh," she moans as Regan begins to move slowly.

"Fuck, I can't," his head tips back, his fingers pressing into her ass cheeks, digging and burying them into her skin as he moves faster, his thrusts becoming harder.

Guy kneels over my chest, I go to reach for him, the need and want to pleasure him is too much but she beats me too it, sucking him deep into her throat.

"Fuck, she looks pretty with every hole filled by us," Guy slams his hips forward.

"You should see it from my view," Regan smirks as he fucks her fast, riding her hard.

Her moans are muffled by Guy's cock, her eyes rolling in the back of her head as she is taken over by pure ecstasy.

"I'm going to nut," Guy pants, and I feel her choke on him. She licks his cock clean and he moves off her, pulling his phone out and filming as me and Regan fuck her.

I wrap my hand round the back of her head and let her tongue slip past mine as I can taste Guy on her tongue, my hips rocking up into her tight cunt as I feel her constrict.

"I am going to come," Regan cries, I break away from

her kiss as Regan lets out a primal growl and orgasms loud as he fills her ass.

He shudders, stilling before he pulls his cock out, rolling on his side as he pants.

"Just me and you now, pretty girl." I lick my lips as I pull my mask off, "ride my cock you little slut, I want to see you bouncing up and down."

Her hands move behind her, gripping onto my thighs as she slips up and down my cock, lifting to the tip before slamming back down. Fatigue flashes through her and before I can ask, Guy and Regan are there. Regan rubs over her clit, fast and hard while Guy sucks on her nipples, kneading them in his large hands.

"Regan," she pants.

"Yes baby," his lips press against hers.

"I want you again," she moans, her head falling back as her eyes roll.

"Let's switch up," I say, lifting her off me as she trembles.

Regan sits against the head board, his hard cock in his hand as he lets his legs drop to the side.

Guy slips a finger inside her cunt, plunging them in deep then smothering Regan's cock in her arousal.

Slipping her down his cock, Regan fills her ass, her legs bent as she leans back into Regan. I lay between his legs and finger her, giving her the best of both worlds before I fill her.

"I will never get enough of this," Regan groans.

"I need her man, I can't fuck her like this." I grit through clenched teeth.

Regan slips out of her and lays her on her side, before taking his place behind her. Guy is there, lifting her leg high, opening her up as I take my place in front of her.

My cock slips into her tight cunt at the same time Regan slips back into her ass. Guy is kneeled between, pushing his fingers deep in her pussy next to my cock and stretching her as her little hand slips between her legs, rubbing her clit.

"I can't, I need you all to ruin me. Stretch me and fill me until I can't be filled anymore," she begs, her body trembling.

"Come for us pretty girl, let it all go," I whisper against her lips as I fuck her like she asked, hard and fast as Regan matches the pace while fucking her ass.

Guy presses another two fingers at her opening, his fingers skimming along the underside of my cock and she explodes, her whole-body convulsing as she lurches forward into my arms, sweat completely covers her as I come inside of her, growling as I fuck her pussy hard making sure my cum fills her deep. I pull out of her and Regan follows, pulling out and rolling her on her back. Pushing her legs wide, my cum and hers drips out of her cunt. Regan swirls his fingers in it and pushes the excess into her ass before he lifts her hips and slams his cock deep inside her ass.

Guy pushes his fingers back into her pussy, rubbing his thumb over her clit. Regan's eyes bulge, his head throwing back as he wraps his fingers around the base of her throat and fucks her ass relentlessly causing an orgasm to rip through her unexpectedly. I lean across, covering her lips with mine to silence the choked sobs that leave her. Regan's grip tightening round her throat causing her to gasp as he fills her pretty fucking ass with cum. Her eyes roll in the back of her head as Regan pulls out, letting go of her throat and she coughs, choking and gasping for air when I pull away from the kiss.

Guy finally slips inside her pussy, groaning as he fucks

her slow. Her hand wraps around my cock as she starts stroking me. Turning my head, I let my eyes fall as I watch Guy's thick cock slip in and out of her tight cunt, and suddenly I need her to myself once more. Guy grits his teeth as he pounds into her, hard and fast, his patience all gone, before filling her with cum. Once he has pulled out, he dives between her legs and licks and drinks every drop of her making sure she is clean. He moves from the bed and she looks fucking spent. She is panting, her hair is stuck to her face with sweat but her eyes are dancing in fire.

"Let me in, just one more time..." I whisper, rolling her on her side and opening her legs as my swollen head presses into her ass, my eyes roll back into my head as I sink my teeth into my bottom lip and ride her tight little ass, filling her to the hilt and fucking her until we're both trembling as our orgasms teeter.

Her cries fill the room, but Regan and Guy are there to soothe her while I continue fucking her ass. Their lips are on her, their fingers trailing and marking every part of her sheen covered skin. I pull my cock to the tip then push into her deep. Letting two fingers slip into her pussy, fucking her with them at the same pace as my cock, her body begins to quiver, her legs trembling and I know she is close again. Her muscles are contracting and tightening around my thick cock as she comes, her loud scream filling the room as I fuck and fill her ass with my cum.

"Happy Birthday, Hallow... I hope it's been everything you have ever wished for." I whisper as I kiss her temple, inhaling her scent before we slip into bed with her and sleep.

CHAPTER NINE
HALLOW

I WAKE HOT AND SWEATY, aching and feeling completely satisfied. I'm in-between Rune and Regan and Guy's head is on my stomach. We slept for a few hours before Regan and Rune fucked me once more before Guy got his turn to really take his time with me and fuck, can that guy fuck. He is slow, sensual, but hits the right spot every single time.

I stretch, lifting my arms above my head. Guy's eyes meet mine, full of sleep and haziness.

"Morning pretty girl," his voice is muffled.

"Hey," I smile as he crawls up my body. His erect, thick cock nudging at my opening, slipping straight into me as he fucks me slow and soft.

My moans begin to leave my lips as my orgasm begins to ripple, Guy grunts and comes inside of me. Smirking, he shakes his head as he covers my mouth but it's too late. Regan and Rune are awake.

"Don't be greedy with our girl," Rune groans, his hands kneading my breasts, his mouth over mine as he kisses me. Guy pulls out, turning me on my side as Regan lifts my leg, wrapping it round his hips as he slips inside of my pussy, and groans in my ear. Guy rubs his fingers over my clit, my whole-body tingling.

"I hope you know pretty girl, you're ours now." He pants, his own cock hard as he nudges his head at my opening.

"Open up, you can take them both," Guy presses, helping Rune slip inside of me slowly and I shudder, my pussy clenching around them. *Fuck.*

"Yours," I pant, my eyes closing as I let the pleasure rip through me from them both fucking my pussy.

"You're never going to be without us again," Regan grits as his and Rune's cocks fuck me slow, both pulling to the tip and sliding back inside in sync.

"I love you, each of you, I always have..." I gasp, my orgasm teetering.

"Not as much as we love you pretty girl," Guy moans, his fingers rubbing faster over my clit and my orgasm rips through me like a freight train, sending me free falling into oblivion.

We didn't move from the bed, each of them spending their time on me, making me come over and over as a group and individually.

It was perfect. I had never felt as consumed by anything than I did them. I had never felt as complete as I did now, I felt whole. Finally.

They were my boys.

My seekers.

I was their girl.

Their Hallow.

My forever.

THE END

ACKNOWLEDGEMENTS

Dan. My best friend. My husband. My world. Thank you for pushing me to start this crazy journey. I love you to the moon and back.

Thanks firstly to Robyn, for keeping me in check and always being there when I needed you.

My girls, our little group. Thank you for the constant support and love you give me. I am so grateful to have you in my life and being with me on this crazy author journey.

My BETA's and friends, Sophie and Harriet. Thank you for being honest and loving my characters as much as I do.

Leanne, thank you for always being here for me. You're a friend for life.

Lea Joan, thank you once again for squeezing this in last minute. You have always been by my side in my author journey and I am so grateful that I get to work with you.

And lastly, my readers... without you, none of this would have been possible.
    My loyal fans, I owe it all to you.

CRAVING HEX

READERS NOTE

This is a little to no plot, pure smut novella. When I say it's filthy, I am not lying. The church scene alone is panty melting... and a little bit naughty...
Forgive me father, for I have sinned.

PROLOGUE

Climbing the steps of Jed's house, I open the front door and stand for a moment as I gaze around the large space looking for him. I see Hex and a group of friends sitting by themselves all smoking a blunt. Hex's eyes burn through me but I ignore the pull to look at him. Marching over I see Jason is sitting with the group, stoned out of his head.

"Where is Jed?" I ask, crossing my arms over my chest but the bonehead says nothing.

"He's upstairs," Hex responds, drawing my reluctant eyes over to him. He licks his lips, his legs open and his arms resting between them as he lifts the joint to his lips and pulls a drag.

"Doing?"

"Why don't you go and see for yourself," Hex smirks, his eyes pinned to mine and I know what he is referring too.

I turn and run for the stairs, climbing two at a time before bursting through his bedroom door to see slutty Cindy bouncing up and down on his cock.

"Shit," his eyes widen when he sees me and my own

eyes sting, my throat burns. Jed pushes Cindy off him and clambers off the bed.

"It's not what you think it is, baby," Jed says as he moves closer to me.

"No? Then what is it? Cos to me, it looks like the boy I'm seeing is fucking some whore!" I scream as the tears roll down my cheeks. "I'm done with you, fuck you." I spit, flipping him off and slamming the door shut behind me as I leave.

Running down the stairs I can't even bear to look over towards my darling stepbrother and the pricks he calls friends.

"Obviously you wasn't enough for him," Hex bites out and I still, nibbling my bottom lip as I close my eyes for a moment. "Don't waste your tears over him, angel. I'll fuck you right and make you forget all about him."

I turn, my fists balled by my sides as I focus my glare on Hex.

"If you were the last person on earth, I would never, ever, lower my standards by fucking you," I growl. "Plus, I'm not into small, pencil dicks," I flip him off and slam the front door behind me.

What an asshole.

CHAPTER ONE
LAUREN

Rolling over, I groan when I see all my boxes piled around my bedroom. I cannot believe I am back living with my parents. This was not the plan when me and Hallow decided to move out and face the big wide world by ourselves. But, alas, we never planned for her to fall in love with her brother's three best friends. They didn't let her out of their sight, and after only a month of dating she moved in with them. It's fine. I'm happy for her, *real* happy. But I am also envious of her. I want someone to love me as much as Rune, Guy and Regan love her. Fuck, she has three hot as fuck guys who are putty in her hands and worship the ground she walks on and I can't even get Jed to commit to me.

I sigh, rolling onto my back as my eyes pin to the ceiling. I needed to get a little job and keep myself busy. I love my mom, but my stepdad is a dick and so is his son. Mom's happy so I have to be happy. He treats her well, so I shouldn't complain but he just seems so entitled and it grates on me.

My eyes widen as I hear muffled moans and the sound of Hex's headboard hitting the wall.

"Fuck's sake," I stretch my arm up and bang on the wall three times which only makes the slut on his dick cry out louder.

Reaching for my pillow, I pull it over my face and hope to smother myself. After a few more minutes of enduring the noise, I give up, getting up from the bed I take myself to the en-suite for a shower. At the least the water running will drown the slut out.

Stepping out of my en-suite a while later, I pull my towel tight to my body and still when I see Hex sitting on the edge of my bed.

"Get out," I stamp my foot.

"Oh, come on darling, don't be like that," he pouts as he pushes his brown floppy hair away from his face. His jaw is chiselled and his cheek bones high. His gorgeous brown eyes roam up and down my wet body and I feel my stomach flip. If you opened a dictionary and looked up the word handsome, *Hex Henderson's* name would be under it.

"I'm not being like anything, I want you out." I stand tall, not budging from the spot I am standing on.

"I thought we could have a bit of brother-sister bonding time." He licks his top lip and lays back on my bed, his elbow resting so he is propped up.

"You're not my brother."

"Technically, through marriage, yes, yes I am."

"I hate you." I spit.

He lets his head tip back and he laughs.

"No you don't," he shakes his head from side to side as he stands and makes his way over to me, his face so close to mine that I can feel his heavy breath on my face. "Tell me, little one... was you fingering yourself over the noises you were hearing this morning? Was your pussy soaked as you imagined it was you bouncing up and down on my cock?" His eyes burn into mine as I hold his steady gaze.

I smile sweetly, pressing my body up against his and trail my fingertip down his chest. His eyes darken, his chest heaving.

"I was fingering myself..." I press onto my tiptoes so my lips are next to his ear, "but not over you, baby. You repulse me." I hear the grind of his teeth as he clenches his jaw. "I was hoping your teeny, tiny dick was going to drop off." I lick my lips and step back, my eyes searing through him.

His hand comes to my face, squeezing my cheeks as he presses me back against the wall.

"I will make it my life's mission to make your life hell, Lauren. I am going to fucking ruin you," he whispers, his breaths ragged. "And I am going to enjoy every second of it."

I spit in his face and shove him off me.

"Go to fucking hell."

He smirks as he wipes the spit from his cheek then snaps his head back towards me and grits his teeth.

"Oh, I will be and after I'm finished with you, I'll be dragging you down there with me."

CHAPTER TWO

TRUTH WAS, I did like Hex. More than liked Hex. There was always something between us and I know he felt it too but the thin line between us was growing thicker and thicker as time went on. It made it worse that he was my stepbrother. It was wrong to even think about what I want him to do to me. I sigh, I was definitely going to hell.

"Darling, are you ready for church?" Mom calls up the stairs and I step back from the mirror. I am wearing a red skater dress that sits mid-thigh. My brown hair is in loose curls and the top half is clipped back from my face.

"Coming!" I call out.

"Not yet you're not," I hear as Hex appears in my doorway dressed in all black like the sinner he is. Wearing a black fitted shirt and black skinny jeans finished with *doc martens*. His brown hair was loose and sitting in curtains that sat just at the side of his temples and all I could think about was running my fingers through his hair while he devours me.

"You're disgusting," I huff as I walk for my doorway. His hand skims across my ass as I pass and he squeezes.

"I will get you my little temptress, mark my words."

"You won't, mark my words," I scowl as I step forward and make my way downstairs.

"You look lovely darling," my mom smiles as she kisses me on the cheek.

"Thanks, so do you," I return her smile but all I can feel is the overwhelming presence of Hex behind me. I step off the bottom step to create more distance and slip my shoes on.

"Hex, you look very smart and handsome," my mom gushes and I roll my eyes.

"Please don't inflate his big fucking head any more than it already is," Hex is big headed; he thinks he is God's gift and people blowing smoke up his ass makes him even more intolerable than he normally is.

I don't give Hex or my mom a chance to respond to my comment as I shoot out the door and climb into his dad's SUV.

"You okay?" Christopher, my stepdad, asks.

"I'm fine," I bite, a little harder than I would have liked.

"Okay Poppet," his eyes move from the rear-view mirror as he turns to watch my mom and Hex walk towards the car. "I know Hex can be a little much, and I know you don't want to be here but if you could just try and get on with him for your mother's sake, I would really appreciate it," he rushes out as my mom opens the door and I let my eyes flick up to meet Christopher's, nodding as I swallow the lump down in my throat.

Hex slips in next to me, moving to the middle seat and I stiffen. Turning my head I look out the window, not interested in looking at him or making conversation with him. We pull off the drive and head towards church. My mom fiddles with the radio and *Take Me To Church – Hozier* plays and I nibble the inside of my lip as Hex's hand slips between my thighs, drawing small circles on my bare skin. This is so wrong. He makes my skin tingle, my stomach knotting and burning as arousal strikes through me, coursing through my veins. Before I realise it I let my legs fall open slightly as he strokes the front of my panties and I sigh, my eyes still watching the sidewalks go by out the window. My hand rests on his thigh, curling my fingers as I dig them into his jeans as he presses harder, rubbing my clit through the lace of my panties.

"Stop," I breathe.

"Why when you're enjoying it so much?" he whispers, just loud enough for me to hear over the music.

"It's wrong." I close my legs tight, squeezing his hand before ripping it away. I chance a glance at him and he brings his fingers to his lips and sucks.

My mouth falls agape, my cheeks heating as I turn to face the window again.

"You're wet for me baby, just admit it."

"Bite me," I snap.

"Oh, I will." He threatens, almost inaudibly and I have never been so grateful to be at church than I am now.

I rush from the car and beeline to the church, being sure to walk ahead with my mom and stepdad.

"Eager are we?" Christopher jokes and I force a laugh. Not eager, just desperate to get away from the devil.

CHAPTER THREE
HEX

I HAVE NEVER WANTED a girl more than I wanted Lauren. From the moment my father introduced us I have wanted her. She is a good girl. I'm a bad boy. We're no good for each other but all I can think about is how I can corrupt her. Jed's a fucking idiot for treating her the way he did but all he is done is make her even more available for me and I won't stop until I have her. I need her in every way possible. My heart drums; she gave me an inch in the car, but now she has shown me that she is as willing as I thought she was, I need to take it even further. I want her bouncing on my cock as I take everything from her.

I stay back and watch as she walks with my father and stepmother thinking that will keep her away from me. She is sadly mistaken.

Our parents greet the priest before making their way to the pews close to the back of the church and I pick up my steps as I close the gap between me and her. If she thinks that after our little car trip I am going to leave her alone than she doesn't know me as well as I thought she did. She just gave me the green light and I intend on taking it.

Slipping past my father and my stepmother, I sit next to her and hear her exhale a heavy sigh.

"I wasn't finished," I lick my lips as I keep my eyes forward.

"Well I was."

"Hardly," I scoff, "you were up for it, don't go back now."

"I wasn't up for anything," she snaps, her voice a little louder than she intended as it echoes round the church, eyes find her and she blushes.

"You so were," I laugh quietly before turning my head and seeing the dagger stares from both of our parents. I shrug my shoulders up and my dad holds two fingers in front of his eyes before twisting them on me and I bite the inside of my lip. Fucking dick.

I shuffle and feel my cock harden at the thought of what I want to do to her, what I am *going* to do to her. Side eyeing her, I listen to the priest who begins rambling off and I yawn.

"Stop looking at me," her voice is low.

"I'm allowed to look, plus, I am bored shitless."

"Then you should have stayed home," her head turns to face me and her eyes narrow, "now be quiet, I am trying to listen to how to eradicate the devil that is haunting me." I see her lips twitch as she fights her grin.

"Oh baby, I'm here to stay. I'm not going anywhere." I lick my lips, my hand moving over her thigh as I rest it there, gripping and digging my fingers into her delicate skin.

"Hex," she breathes, "they're going to see," her eyes widen.

"And?"

"Stop it," she grits, her eyes bugging as she pushes my hand away.

"You're such a spoil sport."

She turns back and faces the front, completely ignoring me which is riling me up as anger bubbles that she won't just admit that she wants this.

I look around the room at all the boring fuckers sitting here nodding along to whatever this guy up front says. They hang on his every word, stupid pricks. Clicking my knuckles my eyes land on Jed who is the only person not hanging onto the priest's words, instead staring at Lauren with a sappy look on his face. I reach up, yawning, then place my arm behind Lauren's back and rest it on the back of the pew and I smile while flipping him off with my spare hand.

Take that you spineless cunt.

Leaning across, my lips brush against the shell of her ear and I hear the sharp intake of breath that she takes. "Jed keeps looking over at you."

She doesn't turn to look; she continues facing forward ignoring me.

I roll my eyes, looking back to Jed and smirk before my lips lower to her ear again.

"How about we give him a little show? Let me show him how much I *want* you."

That gets her looking.

"No," she mouths and shakes her head.

"You know you want to..." I whisper, my fingers tracing over her bare shoulder, and her eyes widen as she looks at Jed who is still gawking at her.

"Show him that you're over him... show him that you aren't upset anymore that you caught him fucking some slut." I whisper, my arm moving from behind her and into her lap as I tap the inside of her thighs, "Let me in." She shudders, parting her legs slightly.

"People are going to see," the panic is evident in her voice.

"No they're not, the only person who is going to see is that tool," I smirk as I slip my fingers between her legs and rub her clit through the thin material of her panties. "You're so wet," I lick my lips and she grips the hem of her skirt, keeping it pulled tight against her thighs.

"Tell me; tell me how long you have wanted this Lauren," I keep my eyes pinned to Jed, not lifting my sight off him for a single second.

"Hex," she breathes as I continue rubbing her sensitive clit, her eyes flutter shut and her head falls to her chest just as the rest of the churchgoers bow their own heads in prayer. All except Jed whose eyes stay locked on us.

"Tell me," I whisper, licking the shell of her ear and her body tremors.

"So long," she breathes, her legs parting further as I hook a finger beneath her panties and sink two fingers inside of her.

"Good girl," I praise, pumping inside then rubbing her clit before gliding my fingers back inside of her, her legs tremble and she tightens her grip on my thigh. I wink at Jed as he watches his ex come over my fingers in the middle of church. Her pussy tightens, clenching around me as she lets out a moan just loud enough for me to hear, and I send out my own little thanks to God that it can't be heard over the prayer echoing through the church.

I smirk, slipping my fingers out of her and pushing them past my lips as Jed watches me with narrowed eyes as I suck my fingers clean.

Everyone stands, and so does Lauren. Her cheeks are

flushed, her chest rising and dropping fast. I curl my fingers round her wrist and drag her to the end of the pew.

"What a lovely service," my stepmother chimes as she leans into my father, his arm pulling her to his side.

"It was, wasn't it," I chew the inside of my cheek to suppress my smile.

"You okay darling?" Lauren's mom asks and she nods.

"We will meet you at home, we're going to go to the diner across the road for some lunch, is that okay?" I ask, putting on my best act.

My father and stepmother look at each other, and no words are exchanged.

"Erm, of course... I suppose?" My father's gaze moves to me before his sights land back onto my stepmom.

"I'm okay with it if you're okay?" she offers, her eyes moving to Lauren and she nods, smiling.

"Well, okay then," my father softly shrugs his shoulders up and takes my stepmom's hand, leading her outside the church.

As soon as they're out of sight, Lauren snatches her hand from mine.

"What are you playing at?" her voice is sharp.

"I'm not playing at anything..." I wink, "yet."

She rolls her eyes and I see Jed heading towards the back of the church and the confession box. Lauren's eyes stay pinned as she watched her mom and my dad walk away.

"Trust me?" I ask, taking her hand I drag her through the church, following Jed.

"What?" she whispers, trying to pull away.

"Lauren, don't fight this... you're soaked, you want this, you *need* this. I promise... I'm doing this for you baby."

Opening the door to the confession box, I close it

behind us. The musky smell fills me and something about it turns me on, the innocence of this church and me being in here with Lauren is making me feel anything but innocent.

Pulling her back to me, I crane my neck round and nip and suck on the skin of her bare throat. She lets her head fall back as my hands skim down her body and grab at the hem of her dress, lifting it and holding it round her waist.

"Take your panties off," I groan, my voice vibrating against her skin as a hint of a moan slips past her lips.

Clearly over denying that she wants this as much as I do, she bends in front of me slightly, hooking her trembling fingers into the side of her panties and slipping them down her long, toned legs. My fingers trail up the inside of her thighs as I slip two fingers inside of her, pumping long and slow thrusts. Bringing them to my lips I suck them dry.

"So obedient," I growl lowly, letting one of my hands entwine in her hair as I tug her head back and lower her lips to mine. Swiping my tongue through her hot and parted lips, my spare hand skims across her skin, her breath catching as I rub her swollen clit.

"Father?" Jed's voice breaks the teasing silence and I feel Lauren tense in my grasp.

"Shh, it's okay," I soothe, dropping my hands from her body as I unbutton my jeans, and sit on the priest's chair. Letting my legs drop open, I fist my hard, swollen cock from my boxers, her eyes widen in delight as she looks over her shoulder and sees I have my dick pierced. Reaching for Lauren, I spin her around and pull her forward towards me. Her legs part either side of mine, and I hold her still.

"How can I help you?" I say softly, her eyes hold my gaze as I push the skirt of her dress high.

"I have sinned," I hear Jed sigh and I lick my lips.

"Go on," I taunt as I rub my swollen head through her slick folds, her breath shaky as I tease her.

"I had a good girl," Jed pauses as I push the tip of my cock at her opening, her head falls forward as I edge her, teasing her. My thumb pad rubs against her clit which causes her hips to rock forward and I groan in satisfaction.

"I messed it all up, I was too coward to commit to her and only her."

"I see," I grit out, clenching my jaw as I hold her hips and slide her down my cock, our skin smacking as our bodies connect.

"She saw me sleeping with someone else," I can hear the thickness in his voice but I don't care, I am too lost in finally fucking my angel. My hips rock up, her hips ride over my cock, her fingers digging into my shoulders.

"And I am saying sorry in advance my lord, for being so crass."

I smirk, leaning forward and nipping her jaw.

"Fuck," she whispers, her hands moving to my face as she rides my cock, my thrusts harder as I spear my cock inside her hot, wet pussy.

"But I have just had to witness her *stepbrother*..." he spits out, as if disgusted by the words that have just left his lips. I grin, holding her hips tight as my finger digs into her skin, while I pound into her. The softness of my thrusts now replaced by full on primal lust.

"Witnessed what?" I rasp, my eyes falling as I watch my cock slipping in and out of her, her tight little cunt stretched round me.

"I witnessed her getting fingered by her stepbrother during your service."

"Well," I lick my lips, her head tipping back and her

hips gyrating over my cock. I can feel her walls tightening as she begins to rub her clit.

"Oh," she moans, not giving a shit that Jed can hear her, and I slide the small panel across so Jed gets full view.

"Now you get to watch me fuck her too," I grit, my head tipping back and resting on the back of the box as I fuck her hard, her body sagging as I take everything I need from her.

"I'm going to come," she cries, her arms reaching behind and resting on my knees as I ride her hard, her head tips back, her lips parting as her pants and moans fill the small area as she comes.

"Look at what you gave up," I spit out so Jed can hear, I know he is still there because the door hasn't opened since. "Watch as my cock fills her; filling her with my cum." I grit, the sound of our skin smacking together echoes in the confined space and she moans.

I roar, burying myself deep inside her and I fill her to the hilt. Panting, I wrap my arms round her waist and pull her into me, cocooning her as I lean forward to look at a wide-eyed Jed.

"Fuck you," I spit, slamming the panel back across and covering her lips with mine.

CHAPTER FOUR
LAUREN

REALISATION SMACKS me in the face at what we have just done, what *I* have just done.

"Fuck," I mutter, my eyes bugging as I climb off Hex's lap and reach for my panties.

"I know, so so good. And that's nothing on what I am going to do to you," he groans as he stands and pulls his jeans up, readjusting his flies and buttoning his pants.

"No," I turn and open the door of the confession box, the smell of sex and deceit surrounding me at me scandalous behaviour.

Hex follows, grabbing my wrist and pulling me towards him.

"What do you mean 'no'?" he grits, his eyes wild.

"Exactly that, what the fuck were you doing?" I spit, pulling my wrist from his vice like grip.

"I thought that was pretty obvious." Smirking, he licks his lips as his eyes trail down my body.

I yank my wrist from his grasp while he is preoccupied and slap him hard across his face.

"Stay the fuck away from me," I shout, my hand

stinging instantly. Rushing out of the church doors, the warm air hits me and I choke as I gasp to fill my lungs.

How could I have been so stupid to give into him; even worse, I enjoyed it.

It's wrong.

So wrong.

I let my stepbrother fuck me in God's temple. If I wasn't going to hell this morning, I was definitely going down there now.

Running down the steps, I begin walking in the direction of home, keeping my head down the whole time. Now I've had the forbidden taste, I crave him so much more. I crave Hex like an addict craves heroine. I was his prey and I willingly gave myself up to him to get back at Jed.

I wasn't this girl, yet all I can think about is when I can give myself to him again. But I can't, it's wrong. I know it's wrong. I need to stay away from him. He is too tempting and now living back home under the same roof it's going to be even harder, but I needed to do this.

I had to stay away.

There was a reason I hated him.

He was the king of manipulation.

And he just manipulated me in the worst possible way. But what was even worse was how I enjoyed every second of it.

The devil made me his own, making my body react in a way it never had before and all I could think about was when he was going to corrupt me again.

Sitting at the breakfast bar in my mom and stepdad's large, manor house my eyes are lowered as I text Hallow telling her what happened.

My stepfather, Christopher, sits next to me and hands me a hot tea with honey.

"Everything okay?" his brow pops and I nod.

"I know Hex can be a little..." He pauses and rolls his lips, his hand rubbing over the stubble on his chin.

"Infuriating? Demanding?" I lick my lips, "*Manipulative?*"

"Well, yes... but that wasn't what I was going to say," he awkwardly laughs while rubbing the back of his head.

"What was you going to say?" I reach for my cup of tea and take a mouthful.

"I just know he can be... a lot." I scoff. "He means well, he has a very hard exterior but once it's broken... then well... he is like a gooey candy," Christopher winks.

"Good to know," I say with little interest apparent in my voice. Christopher senses my brattish mood and walks away down the corridor and no doubt to see Hex.

Hex arrived home about twenty minutes after me, he didn't say two words to anyone as he locked himself in his room.

I haven't seen him since.

Thank fuck.

Sitting at dinner, I push my food around my plate. I don't know why but I feel super shitty about how I treated Hex. I know I shouldn't do, but I do. I can't lie and say I didn't enjoy what we did, but I think I am more annoyed with myself.

My eyes lift from my plate when I hear footsteps hitting the dark, hardwood floor behind me and my heart skips a beat.

"Hexley," Christopher says as he pulls the seat out next to me for Hex to sit down. I scrunch my nose, it's so weird to hear him called by his first name in full. I give in to the pull, turning my head to look at him through my lashes. He is wearing cotton shorts and a fitted white tee, his hair is damp and he smells fresh and delicious. Thoughts run to him in the shower, naked. His thick, large cock being fisted by me, my tongue flicking over his pierced head. I press my thighs together to dull the ache, but my stomach is alight with a burning desire that I can't seem to dampen.

Conversation flows between our parents and Hex's fingertips brush against the inside of my bare thighs, edging towards the hem of my silk short pyjamas.

My breath quivers.

My mom clears the plates, Christopher following and disappearing. I take that as my cue to stand and leave. I am embarrassed by my behaviour and just want to hide away in my room. I press my lips into a thin line as I push out my chair, the legs scraping on the hardwood floor. I ignore the pull to look at Hex; we're no good for each other. Stepping down the hallway, I pace my steps until I round the corner and I bolt upstairs.

CHAPTER FIVE

I LAY on my bed watching *Gossip Girl* and I can't help but love the toxicity between Chuck and Blair, and suddenly, I feel like I am watching myself and Hex on the tele.

I was the 'it' girl, he was the 'it' boy. We clashed, even more so when either one of us were in a relationship. I hated the fact that he was with someone and vice versa. The hate I felt for that boy coursed through my veins like venom and I am sure the feeling was mutual, and yet I still craved his attention, whether it was good or bad.

I sit up when I hear the creak of the floorboards outside my door, my heart thrashing in my chest and my breaths silent.

It's him.

It's always him.

He paces up and down outside the hall before he slips into his bedroom and slams the door.

But tonight, he didn't. He just walked straight past.

Disappointment courses through me when I hear his heavy footsteps pace down the stairs. My heart sinks, I take a moment and I annoy myself that I am letting this bother me so much.

Pressing play on the tele, I fall back into my bed and let the thoughts of Hex leave my mind for an hour or so.

My eyes feel heavy, but I am thirsty. Swinging my legs off the bed, I pad quietly across the large space that is my bedroom and gently open the bedroom door. Sticking my head out, I look up and down the hallway and breathe out a sigh of relief that he wasn't there. Tiptoeing out, I ease down the stairs softly and rush towards the kitchen. I reach up onto my tiptoes and stretch my arm for a glass, my top riding up as I did.

I hear a noise behind me and I still, my skin erupts and my heart drums in my chest. Slowly flattening my feet against the cool tiled floor, I step back cautiously and turn to see Hex sitting near the back doors with a joint hanging from his plump lips. He doesn't move his eyes from mine as I stalk across the kitchen and turn the faucet on, letting the cold water run for a moment before placing my glass under the running stream. I swallow, my mouth dry.

Just ignore him my subconscious reminds me.

Turning the faucet off, I turn on my heel and pace back towards the door of the kitchen. The beat of my heart thrums, skipping beats and making me catch my breath.

"Why are you running *little one*?" his voice echoes down the hallway, and I smirk. I turn to face him.

"Because I can't stand to be near you," I snap, tightening my grip on my glass, being mindful not to shatter it.

"Well, that's not true is it?" He licks his lip, standing

and stalking across the floor to me and exhaling the smoke that he has just inhaled.

"It really is."

"You didn't mind when you were being fucked earlier today," smirking, he takes another long, slow drag. My eyes bug out of my head, swallowing the large lump that seems to be lodged in my throat.

"You used me," I snap.

"Did I? Or did you use me?" he laughs softly, turning is head to the side as he slowly licks his bottom lip, sinking his teeth into it then sucking it behind his front teeth.

"Leave me alone," I snap, "I'm over you. Over *this*. I *hate* you. Today was a moment of weakness." I shake my head, turning on my heel.

"There is a very thin line between love and hate *darling*, and we crossed that line earlier."

"Fuck you, Hex," I flip him off.

"Nah, I prefer getting fucked by *you*." He laughs and I begin to stalk away. "I must admit, Lauren," he calls after me, his voice booming through the empty house. Our parents are out for drinks with their friends. Spinning to face him, I narrow my eyes on his as his hazel eyes roam up and down my body. My sex aches with want and need to be filled by him, to sin once more. "Your bratty behaviour turns me on," he blows smoke in my direction and palms himself with his spare hand through his cotton shorts.

I roll my eyes.

"Are we finished?" I pout, my fingers playing with the frilly hem on my grey pyjama shorts. My ass cheeks hang out the bottom and normally I would try and hide that but I want Hex to see.

"Oh baby, we're only just getting started." He laughs, putting his joint out in the sink and stalking over to me, his head low, his eyes dark as he pins his sights on me. Before I can move, he is standing in front of me, his fingers wrapped around the base of my neck.

"Fuck, you look pretty with my hand around your throat," he groans. Pushing me back towards the corner of the kitchen, my back hits the wall as the glass slips out of my hand and smashes at my feet.

"You silly girl," his eyes sweep down my body as he notices some glass has cut the top of my foot. Bending down, he swipes his thumb over the incision then looks up at me through his lashes and sucks his finger. Gasping, he kneels on both knees in front of me and pulls my shorts to the side revealing my bare pussy. "Fuck," he sucks in a breath, his fingers digging into my thigh. His face edges forward as he swipes his pierced tongue through my slick folds, sucking on my clit. Fuck, it feels *amazing*.

"Hex," I breathe, my hands running through his soft hair as I tug. He lifts my leg over his shoulder, his tongue pressing deeper into me as he lets his tongue glide up and down my pussy.

"You taste so fucking good," he moans, his finger teasing at my opening, "you're such a good little brat, you're going to be my perfect slut." He moans, plunging his finger inside of me.

"You can hate me all you want, but I promise I will fuck the hate out of you…" he continues, his voice drawling, his tongue flicking across my clit before he stops, "because you're mine. We crossed that line and I will never go back." He lurches forward, spreading my thighs as his tongue moves fast over my clit, sucking hard before flattening his tongue and gliding it through my folds as he fucks me with his fingers.

I hear the front door unlock, I freeze, squirming under

his hold as I try to move. He shakes his head, "You better come, slut. Otherwise our parents are going to see my tongue buried deep inside your tight little cunt."

I moan quietly, my eyes falling as he grabs my other leg and places it over his other shoulder. His hands hold onto my hips, pulling my pussy deeper onto his tongue.

"Oh," I moan as the front door closes.

"Quiet Chris, the kids will be asleep," my mom says as we hear her kicking her shoes off, "let's get a drink."

My eyes widen and Hex smiles through his lashes at me, his tongue lashing over my clit, my hips gyrating on his face as I fuck it.

Their footsteps are getting closer, my heart is racing in my chest and Hex is eating my pussy as if it is his last meal. I look down, tilting my pelvis up so I can see the way his tongue is working me and I come, hard. A moan slips past my lips and Hex clamps his hand over my mouth as I ride the orgasm. He drops me as if I've burned him, pulling my shorts back across he stands just as my mom and his dad walk into the kitchen.

"Oh, you're awake?" Christopher says. I can tell he is tipsy, his eyes are glassy and he looks like he has a hanger in his mouth.

"Yeah," Hex smiles, "I just had to get something to eat, I was *starving*." His tongue darts out as he licks his lips. I stand, panting, my chest rising and falling fast as I try to catch my breath.

"What did you have? I fancy a snack," Christopher heads towards the large, double fridge and I feel my cheeks pinch a crimson red.

"Oh, you wouldn't want what I just had... *trust* me." Hex winks at me before walking down the hallway and I stand there stunned. My mom stares at me, and I stand dumfounded. I watch as her eyes move down my body and her brows furrow at the smashed glass on the floor.

"What happened to the glass!?" she tsks, moving to the broom cupboard.

I shake my head from side to side, "Something spooked me, sorry..." I nibble on my bottom lip. "I was just about to clean it up," my hands tremble and I think the shock has hit me.

"It's okay darling," my mom says but she stares at me for a little longer, "are you okay?"

"Honestly? I'm not feeling very well..." I admit, knotting my fingers together.

"Go to bed sweetie, get some sleep." My mom walks over and kisses my forehead.

I nod softly, "Night mom, night Christopher." I mutter, walking towards the stairs and into my bedroom.

CHAPTER SIX
HEX

I LAY IN MY BED, my cock throbbing at the thought of Lauren. I can't get enough of her. I roll and look at the time, it's just gone two a.m. and I know everyone, including Lauren, will be asleep. I could just jerk off, but it's not satisfying enough and honestly, I think I'll give myself dick chaff if I continue fucking myself with my hand.

Pushing off the bed, I pull open my bedroom door and pace outside Lauren's room. I shouldn't, but I'm going to.

Twisting the handle to her door, I pushed it open then closed it behind me. I still, my eyes roaming towards her bed. I step quietly and stand at the end of her bed, my eyes burning across to her and I wait.

Because I know she is going to wake at any second.

CHAPTER SEVEN
LAUREN

I STIR, the feeling of eyes on me sends shivers across my skin. Letting my eyes open slowly I jump, freaking when I see a figure at the end of my bed.

"Don't be afraid brat, it's only me." Hex's voice fills the room.

"Get out," I groan, sitting up.

"No chance, I am horny. I need my dick sucked and I only want you to suck it." Hex's voice is thick, and I lick my lips.

"Get one of your whores to suck it," I scoff, pulling the covers up around my neck.

Hex steps towards me slowly, his hand pushing through his thick, brown hair, moving it off his beautiful face.

"I don't think you understand..." he whispers, kneeling on my bed and fisting my hair as he tugs it hard, tipping my head back. His eyes dart back and forth between mine, his breathing is fast and his spare hand grabs my cheeks as a smirk plays across his lips. "You are one of my whores, and you're going to suck my dick." His tongue pushes through my lips, sweeping across my tongue as he kisses me deep.

Everything wakes up, my senses heightened and I am wet instantly.

My fingers reach out, fumbling with his shorts I tug them down, breaking away and sucking in a breath. I let my eyes fall to his thick cock, and I lick my lips. I eagerly kneel up, crawling forward towards him. I push him back, moving between his thighs and all I want to do is please him like the slut he wants me to be.

My chest heaves as I lower myself, my fingers wrapping around his thick cock. Long, slow strokes cause his head to fall forward, my full lips pursing at his tip, flicking my tongue over his piercing before I take him into my mouth. His hand grabs a handful of hair, tugging at the root as I swallow him into my mouth. Hitting the back of my throat, I gag, my eyes streaming and my throat burning but he won't let me up. He holds my head down, my lips locked round the base of his cock. Stifled moans fill the room, his hips thrusting up.

"Such a perfect little slut," he groans, leaning over me and slapping my ass cheek that's bare under my shorts.

Releasing me, I pull away, gasping for air as my lungs burn. I don't have long before Hex's hand is round the back of my head, his perfect white teeth sinking into his bottom lip as he pushes my head down to please him. I suck him hard, hollowing my cheeks as I let the tip of his cock hit the back of my throat. I gag, but I control it. My eyes begin to fill with tears as he forcefully fucks my mouth. Flattening my tongue on the underside of his thick cock, I swirl my tongue over his tip, flicking across his piercing then putting him at the back of my throat.

He lets out a roar, his hips piston fast as I swallow him and I feel his cock bob as he comes. Pulling his cock from my mouth, he rubs the head of his cock along my cheek. His large hand grabbing my cheeks, he squeezes then runs his tongue across my bottom lip, dipping it inside my hot mouth. Breaking away, his thumb rubs along my lip then drags it across my cheek.

"I am going to have you whenever I want, do you understand?" he asks, leaning forward as his fingers rub through my silk shorts, "Your tight little pussy is mine."

I gasp, his fingers pressing against my opening, the silk rubbing in just the right place.

"Hex," I whisper, my eyes pinned to his.

"Tell me, tell me that you're mine." I nod, his finger pushing inside of me. "Tell me," he groans, his lips pressing to my jaw, his teeth grazing and nipping.

"Yours."

He continues fingering me in a slow and teasing manner.

"Yes you are," he licks my cheek, his hand still gripping my face tightly. Abruptly pulling his fingers from me, he sucks them clean.

"You're such a good girl," he winks, leaning across and kissing me on the forehead. The bed dips as he crawls back and moves from the bed.

"Sweet dreams, little one." He smirks, licking his lips before he is gone.

CHAPTER EIGHT
HEX

It's been two weeks since Lauren sucked me off and my cock still hardens at the thought of it. I had to go away for work and she has been out most of the time and I can't help but think she is ignoring me. My mind runs away and I can't help but worry that she is seeing Jed again. No, no... she wouldn't.

She knows she is mine.

Dropping my keys on the side table I stop in the lobby of the large house.

"Dad?" I call out, "Lily?"

Nothing.

Pulling my phone out I message my dad and he replies that they're shopping. A smirk pulls at the corner of my mouth. Kicking my shoes off, I head upstairs and into my room. Pulling my tee over my head and kicking my pants off I pace for the shower. Letting the hot water run over my body, my fingers trail up the length of my cock. I am horny. Too fucking horny and all I can think about is sinking my cock deep inside Lauren.

Drying off, I pull a cotton pair of shorts on and leave my

chest bare. Tousling my hair, I move to her room and hover outside but she isn't in there. My stomach coils as I rush downstairs.

Pacing into the kitchen, it's empty. Where the fuck is she?

Moving into the lounge, I stare and that's when I see her. I walk slowly and quietly over to see her laying on her front, wearing tight little cotton shorts and a white cropped vest. Her skin is golden, her brown hair in a high, messy ponytail as she reads her book. Her earphones are pushed into her ears and her feet move to the beat of the music. I round the sofa, standing at the foot of it as I lean over, my large hands groping her ass cheek. She gasps, looking over her shoulder as she scowls at me, her brows pinching. My hand kneads into her cheek, rubbing and grabbing.

"Stop," she sighs.

"Make me," I smirk, kneeling on the white leather sofa between her parted thighs. Dipping my fingers between her legs, I rub her through her cotton shorts, her hips lifting, her head resting on her arms. My spare hand slaps her ass; grabbing her hips I pull her up, and push her top half down so she was in the perfect position. I tug her shorts away, pulling them down her legs as my hands spread her ass cheeks.

"Do you know how long I have been *craving* this pussy?" I moan, my fingers rubbing her clit, warming her up.

"How long?" she mewls.

"Since the moment I laid eyes on you, all I have thought about is this." I press my thumb into her soaked opening, pumping slowly as my fingers continue rubbing over her clit. Her eyes find mine over her shoulder, her teeth sinking into her bottom lip.

"This is so wrong," she moans.

"But it's so right," my voice is low as I let my eyes cast down and I watch my thumb slip in and out of her plump, wet pussy.

I slip my thumb from her, pushing her forward as I sink down, levelling my eyes on my next meal. Smirking, I flick my tongue at her opening then glide it through her folds as I swirl my tongue on her clit. Her hips rock forward, her moans sounding heavily.

I slap her ass again, rolling her over and parting her legs wide. Hovering over her, I spit on her pussy and run my fingers through, smothering her with my saliva.

Diving down, I grip my fingers into her skin and let my tongue dance over her clit, the piercing stroking her. She sits up, her eyes watching me.

"Your tongue feels so good," she cries, her fingers rubbing over her hardened nipples, "fuck, so, so good," her eyes close, and I turn my head slightly, my tongue flattening and pressing hard on her clit.

"Hex," she cries, her head falling forward as she watches me again. "No one can know about this," her breath shaky as she whispers. Lowering my tongue at her opening, I close my lips over her pussy and devour her until she is coming and screaming.

I sit on the sofa, pulling my shorts down and fisting my hard cock. I reach for her, grabbing her and letting her hover over my cock as her back presses against my chest.

"I am going to fuck you until you're begging me to stop," I nip at her neck, lining my swollen head at her tight opening. Her eyes widen as she notices the mirror, "and you're going to watch me fuck you," I lick up the side of her neck before sucking on her sensitive skin. "Spread your thighs more," my voice is tight as I restrain myself.

She does as she is told, her hands gripping just above my knees as her pussy lowers.

"Such an obedient little slut," I praise, lowering her down my cock slowly. "Fuck, you feel so good," my eyes roll in the back of my head as she wiggles slightly from side to side to adjust.

Rocking her hips back and forth, my fingers dig into her hips as I lift her up and down, slamming her down onto my cock as I do.

Her eyes are closed, her head tipping back.

"Open your fucking eyes and watch as my thick cock fills your tight little cunt," I groan, "look how you're stretched around me, I swear if I fuck you like I want to I will split your little pussy."

"I feel so full," she chokes, her fingers twisting her nipples. Grabbing her hair, I tug her head back, "Fucking watch me." Letting go of her hair, her head falls forward and her eyes fall to watch as I fill her.

"Fuck," she cries, her words barely audible as I piston my hips into her, "don't stop."

"I never plan on stopping." My jaw is clenched, "lift your legs up, I need to fuck you deeper."

She lifts herself, her feet resting on the leather seat of the sofa. Her hands move back as she grips, steadying herself as she lifts up to the tip of my pierced cock, holding herself there as she clenches.

"Shit," I groan, pulling her hips down on top of me, "do that again," I beg.

And she does, one of her hands skims over her body, dipping between her legs as she rubs her clit, not looking away from the mirror as she watches as she takes my cock deep.

"Fuck me Hex, fuck me like you hate me," she cries and

something snaps inside of me. I lift her off me, throwing her down on the sofa and pushing her head down, holding it there with force as I slap her bare ass over and over again.

She cries out, her perfect ass reddened by my hand. She spreads her legs farther, tipping her pelvis back and giving me a perfect view of her pussy. My fingers rub over her clit before slapping her little nub hard.

"Shit."

"You like that my little whore?"

"Yes," she cries, as I slap her again. "Hex!"

Slap

"Fuck me, please, I need you..." she sobs, and I slap her swollen clit one last time before lining my thick cock at her opening. Slamming into her, I reach forward and lose my fingers in her hair, tugging her up. Her ass is in the air, her back arched as I ride her into the sofa.

"Oh baby," she cries, her cunt clenching around me and she comes, hard. I grit my teeth, letting go of her hair, I press her face into the pillows as I fuck her, I don't know what comes over me but I pull out of her soaked pussy, dipping my fingers in where my cock just was. I swirl her arousal over her asshole, edging a finger in and out of her slowly. Once she is ready, I press the tip of my swollen cock at her tight hole and rock my hips forward, filling her slowly to the hilt and still. I give her a moment to adjust, pulling out to the tip then pushing my hips forward, my cock filling her hard.

She screams, tears filling her eyes as I pull out slowly, edging before pushing back into her.

"I'm going to fuck your ass then spurt my hot come all over your face," I grit as I continue riding her tight little ass. "Please tell me I'm the only one that's been here," my head falls back, my eyes rolling in the back of my head as I hold my orgasm off. Her fingers press and rub over her swollen clit and I feel everything tightening again.

"Only you," she sobs.

"Fucking come for me," I slam into her hard, and she cries out. Pulling out of her, I spin her over, climbing over her torso and pinning her arms down with my knees as I stroke myself fast and hard before exploding over her face. She licks what she can reach, then rubs her fingers in my arousal before sucking her fingers clean.

"Such a good slut."

CHAPTER NINE
LAUREN

Every time I sleep with Hex, I vow it'll never happen again, but it is does. Over and over again.

I lay in the hot bath, the steam filling the large bathroom as I run my fingers up and down the edge of the bath. The hot water soothes my aching muscles, only to be reminded of Hex and how he worked my body up. Desire swirls deep in my tummy, my nipples hardening as I replay the memory of Hex fucking me as I watched. It's purely lust driven. There is nothing romantic about what we do.

We don't laze and kiss after, he fucks me and makes me feel good but then he disappears. My aching need passes as rage consumes me. Standing from the bath I wrap a towel around me and pad across the hallway to my bedroom leaving wet, bubble footprints as I do.

I sit on the edge of the bed letting my over-thinking drive me wild. I lean back and reach for my phone, hovering over Hallow's name I debate calling her, but I can't. No one can know about the sick little secret that happens between me and my stepbrother. It's wrong. It's forbidden, taboo, *sickening*.

My stomach rolls and I throw my phone on the comforter of my bed. Falling back, my fingers grip the top of my towel. I feel exhausted, the hot bath and the hot as fuck sex has knocked me.

My eyes fall heavy as I focus on the ceiling above me, my heart thrums in my chest and my mind is consumed with Hex. It's always Hex. I can't say my thoughts out loud for I have sinned, but in my mind they're safe and locked away. I had fallen for him, hard. The way my heart races when he is near, he lights up the room by just being there and the connection that runs through us is overwhelming. I need him like a drug, crave him like an addict. I finally give in and move from the bed in a heavy, sombre mood. I need to break it off. This isn't healthy and the way he is making me feel, this overwhelming *love* that I feel for him, this overwhelming *craving* that I have to please him and be everything he wants me to be is too much.

Pulling out a silk, white nightie I skim my hands over the material and hang the towel over my radiator.

I turn my phone off and climb into bed alone, until the devil himself turns up to corrupt me and leave.

But not tonight.

It was over.

CHAPTER TEN
LAUREN

I HUM, my mind filled with Hex between my legs, my body reacting in a way it only does with him. I am in seventh heaven. My pussy pulsing, his expert tongue swirling and sucking my clit.

"Hex," I breathe, my body trembling as my impending orgasm teeters on the edge, ready to send me into oblivion.

"I'm right here, baby," his voice soothes my choked sobs.

I stir, realising I'm in a wonderful sex dream and disappointment begins to fill me as I slowly wake to my dark bedroom. I still when I feel an arm draped over me, soft snores breathing down the back of my neck and I smile.

He's here. Rolling over to face him, I take a moment to just gaze at him. Long, black lashes fanned across his cheeks, plump, parted lips allowing his breaths to leave.

"Lauren," he whispers against my ear and my skin erupts in goosebumps.

"What are you doing?" I ask, keeping my voice low.

"I sneak in most nights, you just don't normally know," I see his smile growing.

"Pervert."

"Were you having a sex dream?" his voice is lazy and full of sleep. I freeze, swallowing down as my mouth goes dry.

"No," I whisper, and I am grateful that it is dark as I can feel the burn on my cheeks.

"Then why were you moaning my name?"

"I wasn't," I snap, my eyes widening.

"Stop lying, little one." His voice is raspy, his eyes pinning to mine as his fingers stroke in small circles along my thighs.

"We can't keep doing this," I breathe, my eyes fluttering shut as the growing desire presents itself in my lower stomach.

"I know," he licks his lips before covering my mouth with his soft lips and I melt into him. His fingers continue their trail, dipping between the apex of my thighs and he hums when he feels that I am bare.

"Such a naughty little slut; you're such a cock tease..." my legs part willingly as his fingers find my clit.

"Hex, please," I beg, "we have to stop." My hips buck, my fingers clasping at his bare skin.

"I can't," he breathes, his lips lowering down over mine, "I *need* you, I don't care what people think Lauren. You're mine. You belong to me." He rasps as he sinks two fingers inside of me, my mouth forms an 'o' as pleasure ripples through me. "You will always belong to me."

His lips hover over mine, leaning up I cover his lips as his tongue sweeps through. His kiss is raw, sensual and I feel like my heart is about to explode. Our kisses have never felt like this, this was different.

"I need to make love to you," he chokes, gasping as he breaks away, "I promise I'll fuck you hard and fast after, but right now, I have these unfamiliar feelings suffocating me and all I want to do is fuck you right."

I nod, his fingers press against my lip as he pushes them into my mouth, I suck and lick them clean. Rolling behind me, he grabs my thigh, lifting my leg high as he lines himself at my slick opening, pushing his hips in slowly causing my eyes to roll in the back of my head as pleasure courses through my veins, a blanket of shivers smothers my skin as he stills for a moment.

"I will never get over how good your pussy feels," he groans, his lips pressing into the crook of my neck as he fucks me slow and tender.

"Hex, I," I moan, my finger rubbing over my clit slowly as I match the pace of his thrusts.

"I'm not going to last long, I am too..." he groans, his head falling forward. I turn my head to face him, our lips meeting as his tongue sweeps through my parted lips slowly.

He pulls himself to the tip, his piercing rubbing just where I need it as he fills me slow and deep.

"Shit," I whisper moan into his open mouth, his thrusts getting faster and harder as his fingers dig into the inside of my thighs, "I'm going to come." I sink my teeth into his bottom lip and he turns feral, his tongue stroking mine as our kiss deepens, my orgasm lingering as I ride it. Hex shudders, and I feel his cock throb as he comes, reaching his own orgasm.

"Lauren," he breathes, rolling me on my back, his fingers brushing the hair from my eyes.

"I know," I sob, nodding.

"I love you," his lips press against mine, his fingers gripping my chin.

"I love you, too," I whisper before he lays between my legs and slips inside me again.

Waking in the morning, Hex's head was on my chest, his arms wrapped around me and holding me tight.

"Hey, baby," I coo, my voice soft as I run my fingers through his hair, "we need to get up, it's church."

He groans, lifting his head and his eyes find mine, still full of sleep. "Can't we fuck church off?"

"We can't, we said we would go," I gently push him, "plus..." I chew the inside of my cheek.

"Our parents are going to know that we spent the night together," Hex drawls a lazy smirk.

"We're going to be in so much trouble," I whisper as realisation sinks in.

"We're not, it'll be fine..." he trails off, standing from the bed and picking his jeans and tee off the floor that he must have discarded last night before he slipped in beside me.

"Come," he says, holding his hand out for me to take and I do. I pull a pair of jeans on and a tee. Running my fingers through the ends of my hair, I clasp his hand tightly as our fingers link.

I inhale sharply as my bedroom door swings open, my eyes widening as they land on my mom and stepdad.

"We can explain..." I start but am cut off by my stepdad pulling out his wallet and putting fifty dollars into the palm of my mom's hand.

"What?" Hex laughs, looking down at me before his eyes move to his dad.

"Do you think we're stupid?" My mom's brow sits high, "it's not something we're pleased about... but, who am I to lecture you on who you love?" Her eyes move back and forth between me and Hex.

She smirks, turning and taking my stepdad's hand, moving downstairs. I can't move, still trying to process what the heck just happened.

Hex kicks the door shut, standing in front of me he smirks and I pull my bottom lip between my teeth.

"Fuck church," he growls, launching forward as he grabs me and wraps my legs round his waist before taking me back to bed. "I feel like sinning with you," he winks, falling to his knees and ripping my jeans off me. "Plus, I am fucking starving," growling, he parts my pussy and swipes his tongue through my folds.

He was mine, I was his.

Strangers to enemies, enemies to step siblings, step siblings to lovers.

So wrong together, but yet it felt so right.

My constant craving, my darling Hex.

Here's to our forever and ever.

THE END

ACKNOWLEDGEMENTS

Dan. My best friend. My husband. My world. Thank you for pushing me to start this crazy journey. I love you to the moon and back.

Thanks firstly to Robyn, for keeping me in check and always being there when I needed you.

My girls, our little group. Thank you for the constant support and love you give me. I am so grateful to have you in my life and being with me on this crazy author journey.

My BETA's and friends, Sophie and Harriet. Thank you for being honest and loving my characters as much as I do.

Leanne, thank you for always being here for me. You're a friend for life.

Lea Joan, thank you once again for squeezing this in last minute. You have always been by my side in my author journey and I am so grateful that I get to work with you.

And lastly, my readers... without you, none of this would have been possible.
    My loyal fans, I owe it all to you.

SEDUCING WILLOW

CHAPTER ONE
WILLOW

THREE MONTHS AGO

Hearing my mum scream at my stepdad, I roll my eyes and turn the volume up on the television. I have no interest in listening to her. The best thing to happen to us was that my stepdad, Malachi, caught my narcissistic mum cheating with her tennis coach. She has always and will always be a narcissist. She was horrid to me as a young girl growing up. I wasn't allowed to eat anything remotely unhealthy because no one likes *chubby* girls. I'm glad I never let her cruel words control me. As soon as I was old enough to be out of her witchy grasps then I done exactly what I wanted.

My father died when I was five. I loved him with all my heart, I was a proper daddy's girl through and through. Once he died, my mum only got worse. She was a materialistic, stuck-up bitch.

I said what I said.

She met Malachi when I was sixteen; she knew what she was doing. He owned his own oil company and has not long retired. So of course, now it suits her, she is going to try and take him for everything she can. But Malachi isn't silly. He knew what she was like. Did he love her? Probably. Is he grateful to be rid of her whiney arse? Most definitely. He has wanted a child, and after lots of broken promises from my mum, it was too late.

Selfish fucking narcissist.

"Willow!!" her voice booms up the stairs and echoes off the marble floors.

Pushing off the bed, I skip out towards the staircase and hang over the banister.

"Yes," I flutter my lashes as she stands at the bottom of the stairs, her bony fingers digging into her tiny waist.

"Come, we're leaving."

"I'm not. You might be, but I am staying here."

Do I get on with Malachi? Not particularly, but that's because he is a six-foot five Adonis God. I have to keep my distance. I am grown, nineteen years old and I've had a crush on my stepdad from the moment I laid eyes on him. I know it's forbidden, but it's fine because he doesn't look at me like that. But it's not just him. It's also his best friend Ryker.

He makes boys my age look like adolescent children. It's always been Malachi and Ryker.

"Like fuck you are," she rages, her eyes bugging out of her head. She looks like a skeleton. Cheek bones defined and prominent on her small face. "Get down here at once, young lady."

"No, I am an adult. I am staying here." I smile sweetly at her just as Malachi stands beside my mother at the bottom of the stairs. His dark blue eyes find mine and I feel the familiar flutter that sparks through my body. His black hair is beginning to grey but that doesn't make him any less hot.

"Marina, let her stay. She is no trouble." He looks at my

mum then back up to me and gives me a slow and sexy smile.

I beam, my cheeks flushing red.

"No, she cannot. She is *my* daughter, and she is coming with me." My mum barges into my stepdad and huffs as she walks away, her heels clicking across the floor. "Now hurry up!"

My face falls and Malachi notices, his brows pinch and his jaw clenches tight before he turns and disappears from my view.

I edge towards the stairs, moving down to the middle step and I sit.

"Marina, be reasonable. You can't move Willow away. Her friends and her boyfriend are here, her school is a short walk away. If you take her with you, you'll have to drive her every day and she'll be isolated. Don't do it." His voice is soft, there is no malice to his tone whatsoever.

"I don't give a shit, I don't want her with you."

"You're such a selfish bitch. I am so fucking glad we're done. You're not taking her. I'll see you in court," Malachi bites back; I hear him walk away and of course my mum follows.

"Do you know what, keep the brat." She spits her vicious words and I feel my heart lurch. I don't really care for my mother, but the words still sting.

"You don't deserve her," Malachi hisses as he follows her back down the long hallway of our home.

"Whatever, I will fucking ruin you," my mum turns, slapping Malachi hard against the cheek before storming out.

"Son of a bitch," he groans, rubbing his cheek, the sound of his stubble rubbing against his skin.

"Are you okay?" I call out, not moving from the stairs.

"Yeah," he sighs, coming back into full view at the bottom of the stairs wearing a sky-blue shirt tucked into his suit trousers. The top two buttons of his shirt undone for a more casual look and the dusting of dark hair just peeking through. His eyes find mine and I feel the heat blaze deep inside me.

"I'm sorry," nibbling my bottom lip, I feel awful for putting him in this situation.

"Don't be sorry Willow, you're always welcome here. I am just sorry you had to witness it all." He says with a grimace, his eyes not leaving mine.

"I'm used to it," I shrug, my voice quiet.

Silence crackles between us for a moment and I feel awkward and shy suddenly.

"Are you out tonight?" He asks, and my brows ping high.

"I don't think so," I shake my head from side to side, "not sure I fancy going out."

"I'm going to catch up on the F1 race, want to watch highlights with me and order in?" his hands push into his suit pockets.

"Yeah, that sounds cool." I stand and begin to walk back up the stairs, "I'll be back down soon."

"No rush, I'll wait." His eyes stay fixed on me as they dance up and down my body. I nod, then run up to my room and close the door behind me. My pulse racing as I press my back to my door, my palms pushing into the wood as I let my head rest on the hard surface. I just needed a moment to breathe.

CHAPTER TWO
PRESENT DAY

I STAYED home with Malachi all weekend and blew out my friends like I have every single weekend since my mum left. He thinks I have a boyfriend; I don't. I have someone who is a friend with benefits but now I have Malachi here to myself, I am putting all of my energy into him. Things have been going well, and I always crave his attention. Sure, there's been a few stolen glances and sexual tension but that's as far as it's gone.

Pulling my cotton candy pink hair into a high ponytail, I run my hands down my outfit. Wearing a white, low neck bodysuit and a black skort I finish the look off with black chunky boots. I have work at the little coffee shop in Atlantic Springs. It's a small town and not too far from the city so getting out of this town isn't too hard. I check my make-up and trail my finger tips along my freckles that are scattered across my nose and cheeks. I used to hate them as a kid, but now I kind of love them. Smiling, my heart races at the thought of going down to see Malachi. He has filled every single fantasy of mine, and even when I slept with Hugh, it was always Malachi.

Skipping down the stairs, I hold onto the balustrade as I head down into the kitchen that spans across the back of the house. I can hear Malachi and another voice and my skin tingles.

Walking into the room, both of their eyes land on me. Ryker's eyes widen as he takes in my appearance, my busty chest on show. I'm not a petite girl, I have never been petite. My hips and thighs are thick, I have curves in all the right places.

"Morning," I chime, ignoring the way Malachi swallows hard, his throat bobbing up and down. A small smirk plays on my lips as I reach up for a glass making sure I give them both a little tease of what I have.

Malachi is hot as sin, Ryker is also hot. Ryker is Malachi's best friend; recently single as he can't seem to hold down a relationship according to Malachi.

Malachi coughs, clearing his throat as he picks up his conversation, "So, everything is settled and ready for the court at the end of the month?"

Ah, their divorce. Did I mention that Ryker is also a sexy as fuck judge? Thoughts of pleasuring them both flood my mind, and my desperation is growing. The ache between my legs is a sure sign, my pussy pulsing at thoughts of what they could do to me.

"All settled mate," Ryker's raspy voice makes my skin smother in goosebumps.

I turn, moving for the sink and filling my glass.

"So, Willow, how are you?" Ryker asks, his eyes firmly on my chest. I hear Malachi growl. I smirk, twisting my lips as I shut the tap off.

"I'm perfect, a little frustrated, but nothing I can't sort out myself..." I let my words hang in the air for a moment as I take a sip and wet my mouth.

"Is that so," Ryker lifts his brow as he pushes a hand through his thick, blonde hair.

"Yup," I quip, placing my glass in the sink and grabbing a banana from the fruit bowl, I grip the top gently then slide it between my fingers. Ryker smiles, his tongue darting out whilst Malachi adjusts himself in his trousers.

"Anyway, got to run... I have work." I peel the banana then push it between my full lips while giving them a wink as I walk past and out the room.

"Don't even fucking think about," I hear Malachi roar and I smile.

Work dragged and all I could think about was him. Them. Us. My sights are firmly set on Malachi, but I would love to be with both of them, if only once. It would be a night to remember.

"Willow," Andrea calls me out of my daydream, and I jump. Spilling hot milk down my front I wince.

"Shit," cursing, I drop the small steel jug to the floor and roll my eyes. I tip my head back and sigh in frustration. Looking down, my white bodysuit has started to go see-through, making my pierced nipples evident. Reaching for a paper towel I dab myself but it's no use.

"Look, go home. You finish in fifteen anyway. I'll see you tomorrow," Andrea smiles and waves me off. I feel bad but I also don't think the whole of the shop wants to see my tits.

"Thank you," I breathe, taking off my apron and dropping it in my locker as I head out the back of the shop. Reaching for my cigarettes, I purse the tip at my lips and spark my lighter. I take a deep drag and instantly feel relaxed. It's a terrible habit, but I only smoke when I am frustrated and right now, I am frustrated and tighter than a coil. I need loosening and I don't think my vibrator is going to hit the spot that needs attention.

Fumbling with the key to the front door, I push through and dump the keys on the side table. Kicking my boots off I head through to the kitchen when I hear a moan. My heartbeat spikes as I slow my steps and avoid the kitchen, turning my attention to Malachi's office. The door is slightly open and I stand and watch him. He is sitting in his office chair, holding his phone in his hand and suddenly, I am intrigued. I slip through the gap, careful not to be seen or make a sound. Tiptoeing over, my eyes widen and my cheeks flush with heat as I watch Malachi pleasuring himself over a picture of me.

My steps falter and I hit my back on the bookshelf in his room making a bang echo through the room. His head whips round, his eyes bugging from his head and he pushes to his feet, fumbling to do his trousers up as quickly as he could.

"Willow," he stammers, stepping towards me then stopping. His large, frustrated hand pushes through this thick, luscious hair. His cheeks glow red and I don't think I have ever seen Malachi embarrassed before.

"Hey, it's cool. Sorry I should have knocked. Please, it's fine," I nod, my voice quickening as I feel my own embarrassment creep over me. Moving to the side but not taking my eyes off him, I move to the study door and run for my room.

Shit.

CHAPTER THREE
MALACHI

WHAT THE FUCK was I thinking?!

She is my stepdaughter. Or I guess *was* my stepdaughter once the divorce is final. I shouldn't be thinking of her the way I am, let alone doing things and thinking of her.

But I can't help it.

She is forbidden fruit, and forbidden fruit always tastes the best.

My fantasies must remain fantasies.

I can't go there.

She doesn't see me that way and I shouldn't see her that way either.

CHAPTER FOUR
WILLOW

It's been four days since I caught Malachi. I've tried to act normal around him but he keeps quiet and shuts me down at every given moment. I want to scream and tell him that he makes me feel the same way but he won't even give me a chance.

I've blown my friends out again and it's getting to the point where they will stop asking me soon. I debated calling Hugh to come over and just fuck me, but he never seems to satisfy my needs. Heck, I don't think anyone could satisfy my needs.

Reaching for my phone, I hover my thumb over Hugh's name for a moment and quickly decide against it when I hear Malachi and Ryker laughing. My pulse quickens and I drop my phone onto my duvet. Pushing from the bed I look in my full-length mirror and let my eyes scan up and down my attire. I'm wearing a peach silk vest and short pyjama set. The silk shorts have a frilly hem and sit slightly higher over my firm, round butt and letting the crease of my bum hang out. The top is baby doll style, flowy and light and the frill that encased my full chest matched the silk frill on my shorts. My pink hair is down and in loose waves, my face bare of make-up with only the redness on my cheeks from being flustered on show. I was nervous, but excited. Did I tease? Maybe. But I couldn't help myself.

Inhaling deeply, I headed downstairs and followed their voices, my skin prickling in goosebumps. They were sitting in the large lounge, whiskeys in one hand, cigars in the other. Both of their heads turned in my direction, Ryker's smirk growing as his eyes widened in delight and Malachi's jaw was tightly clenched, no doubt grinding his back teeth.

"Hey," I breezed through and stood next to them both, "may I join you?" I ask, fluttering my lashes at my stepdad. He gives one little nod before turning his attention back to Ryker.

Ryker doesn't move, his eyes sweep up and down my body as if he is taking every single part of me in. I blush under his heated gaze. His tongue darts out as he licks his lips in a slow and teasing manner and I feel the pulse vibrate through my core.

"Drink?" Ryker asks, standing and reaching for an empty glass.

"She's barely legal," Malachi grits, his fist balled.

"But she *is* legal, besides one won't hurt surely," he raises his brow at Malachi and he shakes his head.

"I don't want one, regardless my stepdad's input I'm not much of a drinker anyway." I refuse politely, turning my attention fully to Ryker now. If Malachi isn't going to give into what we both want, then I know someone who will.

Stepping closer to Ryker, I run my fingertips up and down his strong, muscular arms that are tucked under a tee.

"I must say, Ryker..." I taunt, still gliding my fingers up and down, "you're a flirt," I giggle and drop the contact.

"Oh, that I am," he winks, taking a mouthful of his whiskey and pinning his eyes to Malachi who glares down at him. "But then so are you," he counters back and steps towards me, "you don't think we know what you're doing in your little skimpy outfits and cute, heated looks towards both of us?" he licks the corner of his mouth. I swallow, pressing my thighs together to try and ease the pulsing between my legs, the growing arousal that I am sure is showing on my peach silk shorts.

"Are you thinking what it would be like to have our thick, hard cocks slipping in and out of your tight little cunt, Willow?"

I gasp at his filthy mouth, my whole body tingling with feelings that I have never felt before.

His eyes trail down over my heaving chest and land between my thighs.

"Look how wet you are already, and I haven't even touched you." Ryker stalks towards me, his arm wrapping around my back and pulling my body against his. His lips edge towards my ear as he deflects his gaze to Malachi, "If he isn't going to touch you, then maybe I can show him what he is missing," his voice trails off as the hand that's on my back skims down, past my bum and under. My whole body heats. His fingers rub over the most sensitive part of my body, slowly caressing me through the silk material that is stopping him from getting to what I want him to.

"So, fucking wet," he growls as he continues. "Look at him," Ryker orders and I do. My eyes move to Malachi who hasn't moved from his spot, it's as if he is cemented to the ground. Anchored even.

My fingers dig into Ryker's shoulders as his lips brush against my jawline as a small moan leaves my lips. His fingers hook inside my shorts and rub over my swollen clit.

"Fuck," I whisper as my eyes stay on Malachi.

"Do you know how long I have wanted you, little one?" Ryker says through his hot, wet kisses.

"No," I breathe.

"Let me show you."

CHAPTER FIVE
MALACHI

My eyes burn into Ryker. I have never wanted to hit my best friend more than I do now. He knows what he is doing, he is pushing my control to its limits. My fists are clenched as I watch him lead her to the sofa, pulling her onto his lap. His lips are on her neck, his hands roaming up and down her curvaceous body. My cock is hard but I am trying not to think about what is happening. I am trying my hardest to block this all out, but her sweet as fuck moans that are filling the room are too irresistible to ignore.

He pulls at her silk top, freeing her full, pert breasts and rolls her hardened nipple between his fingers. His eyes flick up from her, smirking a devious smile against her neck as his eyes pin to mine.

"Look how much he wants you, but he has convinced himself that he can't have you. That you're forbidden. He is probably beating me black and blue in his head for having you the way he wants..." he trails off and licks her neck while squeezing her nipple hard which causes her head to fall back as she cries out. "Let's give him a show baby."

He pushes her off him, unbuckling his belt and pulling

his jeans down. His long, hard cock springs free as he holds himself at the base and I watch Willow's eyes widen. Ryker leans forward, pulling her shorts down in one, swift move. My eyes fall to her bare, glistening pussy. Her arousal is smudged at the top of her thighs. Ryker grips onto her hip with one hand and plunges two fingers into her soaked cunt. She moans, her eyes rolling in the back of her head as he fucks her hard with his fingers. His teeth sink into his bottom lip as he watches.

"Malachi, you're such a stubborn old fool," he groans as he slips his soaked fingers out and pushes them past his lips, rolling his eyes in appreciation at her taste and I feel myself salivate. I am fucking jealous.

He widens his legs, his hard cock erect and ready as he pulls her back onto him, filling her to the hilt and not giving her a chance to adjust. His jaw is locked, his eyes pinned to me as he lifts her up and back down onto him, each time her moaning louder.

"Touch yourself little one, make Malachi watch as you come over my cock," her shaky hand skims down her body as she rubs over her sensitive clit, her hips rotating over his cock as she lifts herself a little higher, then sliding down onto him.

Her beautiful eyes find mine, her lips parted as she pants, her glorious tits bouncing as he fucks her hard.

It's not long before her eyes roll in the back of her head as she cries out, her orgasm exploding around her. Ryker stills, panting as he lifts her off him.

"Get on your knees," he orders and she does, her whole body trembling as she comes down from her high. He grips her hair, tugging her head back and stands over her as he finishes himself off, spurting his hot cum over her face and chest with a proud as fuck smirk.

He rubs his arousal into her chest before thumbing the cum on her face past her lips. She sucks his thumb clean and he gives her a wink. Helping her up, he pushes his lips onto hers, their tongues dancing with each other. Ryker breaks away, bending and giving Willow her shorts.

"Now be a good little girl and go clean yourself up," he slaps her butt cheek hard, the crack of his hand on her skin echoing round the room. She nods, before looking at me over her shoulder and scarpering away upstairs.

He stands, doing his jeans up. He walks towards me, pushing his fingers under my nose.

"That's about as close as you'll get to tasting or smelling just how divine she is," he smirks before pouring himself a glass of whiskey. "You need to get over it, she wants you and you want her... and her pussy is to die for. I'm going to eat her out once she comes back down, I am *famished*."

I grunt, turning on my heel and heading towards the back garden. I need some air. I need a fucking breather.

CHAPTER SIX
WILLOW

THE WEEK WHIZZED by and my stomach fluttered knowing that Ryker was back over tonight. I wanted him, but I also wanted Malachi. I really thought after he saw Ryker fuck me that it would make him change his mind, but I guess not. He has avoided me at every opportunity and I'm getting a little sick of it.

I dressed in a short, pleated skirt and white shirt with the buttons opened at the top giving them the perfect view of my cleavage. Ryker wanted role play tonight, so role play he is going to get. Pushing the pretend plastic glasses up my nose, placing one of Malachi's ties under my collar and tightening my pigtails I head downstairs. My heart thumps in my chest as I get closer. Tonight, they're in Malachi's study. Standing outside the door, I can hear their low voices but not enough to work out what they're saying.

Inhaling deeply, I push through the door and slip straight into role play mode.

"You wanted to see me, sir?" my playful tone gets their attention, and they turn to face me. Their eyes roam up and down my body and I flush under their penetrative stare, loving the attention being on me.

"Yes, I did," Ryker leans round and places his glass on the desk, "I'll be honest Willow, this is becoming the best part of my week."

"I'm glad; shame Malachi can't say the same," my frosty glare moves across to him as I give him a tight smile and he drops his eyes to the floor.

"Well, more fun for me," Ryker licks his lips, "and I must say, Willow, you understood the assignment. My cock is hard as fuck for you." I watch as he rubs himself through his suit trousers.

"How can I help, sir?" my doe eyes widen as I step towards Ryker. His hand reaches out, grabbing the black, silk tie and pulling me towards him.

"You can help by sinking to your fucking knees and helping me loosen the tension from my *busy* day. I've had to deal with brats all day..." his eyes hooded as I fumble with the belt of his trousers and pull them halfway down.

"You're a little brat aren't you, Willow?" He asks as his hand rubs and gropes my ass cheek.

I nod too eagerly.

"And you're bare underneath this little skirt, are you trying to be a tease?"

I blush.

Pushing my skirt up and over my hips he leans back onto the desk, legs parted as he waits for me.

I ignore his command of getting on my knees and place my hands on his thighs as I bend over and take the tip of his thick cock into my mouth, moaning as I swallow him down.

"Yes," he hisses before slapping my arse cheek hard, "you disobeyed me, *brat*."

Pulling him to the tip, I look up at him through my

lashes before hollowing my cheeks and pushing him to the back of my throat.

"Fuck," he groans, his fingers hooking inside my shirt as he rips the buttons open, making them pop across the floor. His harsh hands grope and squeeze my full chest as pleasure swarms him. I feel a hand wrap around my hip and my insides heat, my pussy aching from just his touch. *Malachi.*

"Couldn't resist any longer?" Ryker asks Malachi.

"No I fucking couldn't," his voice is gruff as his hand rubs over where Ryker slapped before he spanks me hard.

"She likes being spanked, her tight little pussy is glistening," Malachi groans as he does it again making a muffled moan leave me as I suck Ryker's cock. I take him deep, pushing him to the back of my throat before I bring him out. Spitting on his head, my thumb rubs over the tip of his cock, spreading his arousal and my spit over him. My salvia is running down the underside of his dick so I run my tongue from his balls all the way to the tip then put him back past my lips and into my hot mouth.

Malachi stands behind me as three thick fingers push into my soaked opening and I tense, wincing as soreness rips through me.

"Relax baby, if you can't take my fingers there is no way you'll be able to take my cock," he leans across my back and whispers, causing a shiver to dance up and down my spine.

Slowly pulling his fingers to the tips, he holds them there for a moment before pushing them back into me. The delicious squelch proving to them just how wet I am for them both.

Ryker's hand grips my pigtails, yanking my head back so my back arches. Malachi pulls his fingers from me and I hear his knees hit the floor. His strong tongue sweeps through my slick folds as he dives into my soaked opening, both hands gripping my ass and Ryker holds me in position as Malachi eats me out.

"Malachi," I moan, my stomach tightening, my pussy clenching.

"Tell us what you want little one," Ryker says, his hand stroking stray bits of hair out of my face.

Malachi slips out, pushing three fingers back inside of me, Ryker's spare hand reaches under me and rubs my clit.

"I'm going to come," I whisper, pleasure suffocating me. My eyes roll and I see fucking stars as I come hard.

"Her fucking arousal is running down my wrist," Malachi groans as he continues to fuck me with his fingers as I ride my orgasm out.

Ryker helps push me up onto shaky legs.

"We're only just getting started baby," Malachi whispers in my ear causing my skin to erupt.

Yanking the zip at the back of my skirt, Malachi pushes it down my legs and helps me step out of it. Ryker is in front of me, pushing my ripped shirt off my shoulders and letting it fall to the floor.

"Put your foot on the desk," Malachi orders and I do. Ryker is in front of me, his fingers digging into my hip as Malachi moves behind me. His fingers trailing through my pussy as he swirls his fingers in my arousal. Ryker widens my stance slightly as I hear Malachi's trousers fall. I clench, anticipation dancing in my tummy. Malachi's hand wraps round my throat, his lips pressing against my jaw.

"All I have thought about is fucking you raw," he whispers. "How your tight little pussy would feel and look whilst full of my cock," another kiss planted, "how you would sound screaming my name as I slam in and out of you," he nips now, his voice growing gruff.

Ryker's fingers find my clit, rubbing softly, his lips moving across my collar bone and down to my hard nipples. Taking one into his mouth, he slowly sucks and licks as I feel a burn.

"Relax baby, otherwise I'm not going to fit," he groans nudging slightly, the tip of his large cock pressing into me, stretching me.

"Fuck," I cry, as I fall forward but Ryker is there holding me up.

Malachi's grip moves to my hips as he holds me in place, rocking a little more so his dick fills me slightly more.

"It's not going to fit," I sob, clenching around him.

"Oh baby, it'll fit," he groans as Ryker continues to rub me. I pant, the feeling of Malachi filling me is overwhelming. He is so thick and long. "There we go; such a good little brat," he groans, slipping out slightly and rocking up into me slowly while I adjust to being full of him.

"Fuck, her pussy looks so fucking good and full," Ryker whispers before sucking my nipple into his mouth while his fingers work me up.

"She feels so fucking good," Malachi agrees as he pulls out to the tip and thrusts his full length back into me.

"Shit," I moan, my head falling back onto Malachi's chest, "your cock feels so..."

I can't even fathom the words, he feels incredible.

"I know baby," he soothes, fucking me slowly while I get used to the feeling.

"I need more," I choke, even though I feel like I am stretched to my limit, I need him to fuck me hard. "I want you to fuck me Malachi," I beg, "I want you to fuck me hard so all I can think about tomorrow is how sore I am, because you ruined me."

I hear as he sucks a deep breath in through his teeth but he doesn't stop, he continues fucking me slowly even though I can tell he is losing his restraint.

"You will take me like this until I say you're ready, do you understand?"

I nod, wrapping my arm around his neck to steady myself against his tortuous pace.

Ryker trails his kisses down my sternum, my navel, my hip bones and pelvis before he bites and sucks my clit into his mouth. His tongue flicking slowly over my sensitive nub.

"Oh," I moan, my pelvis rocking up to meet Malachi's thrusts, but to also get Ryker's tongue deeper.

"You're a greedy little slut," Malachi growls, "but you're my greedy little slut."

I nod, my fingers squeezing and rolling my nipples.

"Stop," Malachi orders and Ryker falls back to his knees as Malachi slips out of me and I wince.

"Come," he orders, taking my hand and leading us out of the study.

CHAPTER SEVEN
MALACHI

I AM ready to fucking explode. I have fantasised about fucking my nineteen-year-old stepdaughter for months. I know it's wrong, she knows it's wrong but to us, it feels so fucking right. I will never let her out of my grasps. She is mine and Ryker's.

Leading her upstairs and into my bedroom I sit her on the edge of the bed before dropping to my knees. Parting her pussy lips, I swipe my tongue up and down her core, swirling my tongue over her clit and sucking. Pressing one, then two, then three fingers inside of her, easing them in gently this time as I work her back up, letting her body make her sweet lube so that she is ready for me to fuck her hard. Ryker climbs on the bed and sits on his knees before swooping down and slipping his tongue in her mouth, kissing her while I devour her. I don't want her to cum, I just want her ready enough for what I am about to do.

Her pussy clamps around my fingers, her legs beginning to tremble. Whipping my fingers out of her, I lean up, breaking Ryker and Willow's kiss and push my fingers into her mouth.

"Taste yourself baby girl, see why we're so addicted to you," I rasp, fisting my aching cock as I stroke myself softly. She moans, her hips bucking for more.

"Patience," I wink, leaning off her, I sit on the edge of the bed next to her. Curling my finger, she sits up like the obedient little doe that she is. Patting my lap, she straddles her legs over my thick thighs, and I grip onto her hips. She gyrates her hips back and forth over my cock, getting the friction she so desperately craves.

"Such a greedy little whore," I wrap my hand in her hair and tug her head back as I suck and bite her neck.

"Please Malachi," she begs, her whines filling the room as she continues moving.

"How much do you want me?" I tease, her head still pulled back.

"Too much," she pants, her arousal dripping out of her.

"I don't believe you," I nip at her cheek, Ryker is in front of her, twisting her hardened nipples.

"Malachi, please," she sobs as I reach my hand down her sweat covered skin, opening my legs wider and slap her clit and she cries out.

"Beg me," I dip a finger in her hot, soaked cunt teasing her as Ryker locks his lips round her nipple, twisting and rolling the other between his fingers.

"Please," she chokes as I pull my finger out and she shudders.

"Not good enough," I do it again.

"Fuck me," her voice cracks as I slip my finger out.

"More," I growl, sinking my teeth into her jaw the same time my finger fills her.

"Please fuck me, Malachi," hot tears roll down her face, and Ryker is right there swiping his thumb pad across her cheek and wiping her tears away.

"There's my good girl," I praise her, lifting her up and pushing her onto her knees as she hovers over me.

Lining myself at her opening, I press my engorged head into her tight cunt, sliding her down me in one, slow, swift move.

Her hands move behind her, gripping onto my thighs to use me where she needs me. Her pussy moves up and down my cock, my thrusts meeting hers.

"Look at my cock filling you, princess, watch me fuck you," I whisper in her ear and nod towards the mirror that's in front of us. Her head falls forward, her eyes widening as she watches.

"Fuck," she pants, Ryker is back on her nipples, twisting and licking them. Ryker moves to the bed, kneeling and grabs her cotton candy pink hair, turning her to face him as he forces his hard dick into her sweet little mouth.

"Look at you getting filled by two men twice your age," I groan, watching as my cock slips in and out of her tight pussy with ease now. "I hate the fact that you've let someone else fuck you," I continue as she gags on Ryker's dick, but he doesn't stop. He relentlessly fucks her mouth, not giving her a chance to come up for air.

"Did they fuck you like we did?" I continue and she moans loudly, "Did they work your body the way we do?" My pounds into her get harder now, the sound of our skin hitting together, her tight little pussy stretched around my cock, and I am sure if I go any harder I am going to split her in fucking two.

"I am going to erase any memory of another man that has been inside you."

Pound. Pound. Pound.

Ryker grips her hair, tugging her head back as he lets a primal roar rip through him and shoots his hot, sticky cum over her face. I smirk as I feel her whole body tighten, her hips grinding down on me, her pussy clenching as her moans grow louder.

"Malachi, oh, shit," she grits, her fingers digging into the skin on my thighs.

"That's it baby," I groan, my own orgasm teetering, "come for me, come all over my cock," I whisper against the shell of her ear and she explodes as my cock slips in and out, but hitting her deep as I come deep inside of her.

We still, both panting, both catching our breaths before I lay her down. Ryker is between her legs, swirling his fingers in her arousal he pumps his fingers and our cum back inside of her.

"Don't want to waste any of this now do we," Ryker winks then lays over her, pushing her knee up close to her chest and pushing into her fast and hard.

"Now it's my turn," he mutters through kisses and I sit back and watch as my best friend fucks our girl.

Our girl.

CHAPTER EIGHT
WILLOW

I WAKE SUDDENLY, slightly startled when I open my eyes. I'm in Malachi's room. My racing heart slows when I turn my head from side to side to see that I am between Malachi and Ryker. Entwined like vines, their legs and arms locked with mine. I move slightly, trying to free my arms and an ache rips through me, my core throbbing with soreness. They definitely weren't gentle last night. A smile creeps onto my lips and I sink my bottom teeth into it.

"Good morning sunshine," Malachi's raspy voice awakens my senses.

"Morning handsome." I twist slightly and place a soft kiss on his lips. His large hand skims over my curves and cups my sex, and I wince.

"Sore?"

"So sore," I blush, nibbling the inside of my lip.

"Don't blush baby, we took a lot from you last night," he leans in, kissing the tip of my nose then throws the duvet back softly and pads out of bed. I pinch my brows as he holds his hand out for me to take. "Come," he smiles.

I lower myself in the warm bath that Malachi run for me, the smell of camomile and lavender fills the room from the oil. Wincing as the water covers the sensitive part of my body, I soon relax once I am under.

Malachi is already naked and stepping in behind me as his large frame cocoons around my back. Water splashes over the edge as he pulls me back into him.

"Let me wash you," his voice is low, his breath smothering my skin in a blanket of goosebumps.

He washes every part of my body gently, his fingers brushing over my sensitive and swollen clit. And even though I am sore, I need him. His erection pushes into my back and I know he wants it too. I push onto my knees, straddling him.

"Baby, what are you doing?" he groans, his eyes dark and full of desire.

"Fucking you," I whisper, as I hold onto the edge of the roll top bath, lifting myself up and watching as he lines himself at my soaked opening. Pressing the tip into me, I gasp at the sting that zaps through me but I don't care. Lowering myself down slightly that's all I can take. Rocking my hips forward to try and take more when I accept defeat.

His fingers dig into the skin of my hips as I use the bath as my support, leaning back slightly as I lift myself up and down his thick, long cock.

"Fuck, your dick feels amazing," I choke as my head tips back.

"You were made for me and Ryker, the perfect mould and we will continue breaking you until we fit perfectly together," his words fall on deaf ears as I immerse myself in pleasure. The water splashes around us as Malachi helps move me faster for his own needs.

"I'm not going to last long," I pant as I let my eyes meet his.

"I want to feel you come baby, just tell me when," his eyes fall from mine as he watches his perfect cock slip in and out of me with ease, my arousal coating his length.

"Fuck," I sob, the feeling too much as he lowers me so I'm taking more of him.

"I know baby, I know," he soothes as his jaw clenches. He swipes a thumb over my clit and my pussy throbs.

"So close," I whisper as he does it again and I crash and burn, free falling into my own pleasure pool.

"Yes baby, let it go," he grits, slamming me down onto him so he is completely inside of me, the water moving with his thrusts as he fucks me hard and fast, filling me to the hilt as he reaches his own release.

"I am obsessed with you," he murmurs placing kisses over my sensitive skin.

"Not as much as I am with you," I lean into him, his arms enveloping me as I kiss his chest.

"Not possible," he whispers, "I love you Willow," and I feel my heart swarm in my chest.

"We both do," Ryker's voice crashes through as he walks towards the bath, his mouth covering mine before his tongue swipes through, "we love you Willow," he breathes.

CHAPTER NINE

A month has passed. A blissful, beautiful month. Malachi and Ryker had made it very clear that I was theirs now. Ryker had been living with us for the last couple of weeks and we've fallen into a routine. Malachi has been a little more tense this week as he has the court case with the bitch that is my mother. I haven't heard from her since she walked out, and I will always be grateful that she is out of my life. I don't care if she was on fire, I wouldn't put her out. I would watch and let her burn. She has never been a mother to me.

"Morning beautiful," Malachi says as I walk into the kitchen and grab a cup of coffee that is just freshly brewed.

"Morning Princess," Ryker's cool tone sweeps over me and I smile. We had the best night last night, just some one on one time and it was needed.

"Morning my handsomes," I smirk, "I know that's not a word but..." shrugging I take a mouthful of my coffee. I stop in front of Malachi and place my hand on his chest. His haunted eyes find mine, they're dark and hollow from the lack of sleep.

"Baby, you've got this. She cannot and will not get anything from you," I cup his cheek and smile at him but he doesn't return the smile.

"I don't care about any of that," he inhales, "it's you I care about, what if she comes back for you?"

"She won't even get close," my voice is soft and gentle, "I'm not going anywhere unless it's with you two, my loves." I try my best to reassure him. "She has nothing, I am an adult, she cannot take me away from you two. Ever."

He wraps his arms around me and pulls me into a tight hug. His lips press to the top of my head.

"You're mine tonight, okay?" he mumbles into my hair.

"Of course," I nod as he lets me go, "I've got to go, I've got work."

"Why don't you just quit, you don't need to work," Ryker steps forward, taking a mouthful of his drink.

"Because I don't want to, I need to do something other than sitting around the house waiting to be fucked by my two hot as God boyfriends."

"Well, I think that sounds perfect, you ready and waiting on your knees for us," Ryker's slow, sexy smile flashes across his face and my stomach tightens at the thought. "Don't you agree Kai?"

He nods.

"You look so pretty on your fucking knees," he hums as he hooks his arm around my back and pulls me into him.

I wink, pressing onto my toes and kissing him on the lips.

"Any requests tonight, my love?" I twist out of his hold because if I don't, I'll never leave for work.

"Surprise me, but I want your hair down."

"Got it," I wink, placing another kiss on his lips, "bye handsome," I whisper and walk towards Ryker.

"Bye baby," I kiss him, handing him my coffee cup.

"Bye Princess, the thought of you from last night is on replay in my memory." He winks and I blush.

Grabbing my bag from the hallway, I slip out the door.

Stepping out the bath, I wrap the towel around myself and pad towards my wardrobe. I scan through my dress up outfits but nothing is calling to me. Sighing, I drop the towel to the floor and brush my hair. It's long, sitting just by my ribcage. I catch a glimpse of myself in the mirror and look at my body, smiling. I have never loved myself more than I do now and it's all thanks to them. My guys.

Walking downstairs, the house is dark and quiet. Ryker is out with friends and I thought Malachi would have been home by now. Pushing the door open to Malachi's private study, I tiptoe in and look around. The bookcases fill one side of the room, there is a mahogany desk and in the corner is a black, grand piano. Smiling, I step over to the piano and run my fingers over the edge.

Sitting on the stool, I press a couple of the keys, the noise echoing round the room. I jump when my phone buzzes. Turning it over, I see it's Malachi.

> Be home in ten, sorry baby.

I smile.

> That's okay, I'm ready and waiting… Sir.
> Come and find me.

Placing my phone on the top of the piano, I climb and

sit on the edge of the cover. My legs wide open, my feet resting on the edge of the keys.

This is where I want him to take out his frustration and release. To take it out on me in any way he wants.

Because I am his.

CHAPTER TEN
MALACHI

Unlocking the front door, I throw my keys on the side. The house is in darkness and my heart hammers against my chest.

Where is she?

Closing the door, I walk slowly and quietly down the hallway sticking my head round every door when I get to it. My heart rate continues to thrash when I hear the sound of my piano. Smiling, my steps grow faster as I head towards where she is waiting. The door is slightly ajar and I push it open, my eyes widening in delight as I see her sitting and waiting.

"Welcome home," she licks her lips as the low light of the room sets the mood.

My cock is hard in an instant. My princess is sitting there, legs wide, completely naked and waiting for me.

"Well, what a fucking treat," I groan, unbuttoning my shirt as I pad over to her, my cock aching between my legs as my arousal beads at the tip.

"Do you like?" she smirks, her eyes on me as she presses

the palms of her hand behind her and onto the high gloss top of the piano.

"Very fucking much."

"Good, all I want to do is please you, sir," she bats her lashes and her big, doe eyes are wide with glee.

"You always please me, little one," I admit, sitting on the stool in front of her.

"Have you eaten?" I ask, my hands gripping her thighs, digging my fingers into her hot skin.

She shakes her head. "I'm not hungry," she pants, my eyes falling to her beautiful, bare cunt that's glistening.

"Good, because I am fucking starving and what I want to eat is right here in front of me," I groan, edging forward and tugging her towards me so her peachy ass and cunt are hanging off the lid of the piano and right where I want them.

"Malachi," she moans as I swipe my tongue through her slick folds, one of my hands pressing against the bare skin of her pussy, pushing on her pelvis as I hold her down. Kissing over her sensitive clit, I drag my lips over the inside of her thigh as my fingers massage her clit, her head falls back as she moans.

"You're such a good girl," I praise her, my lips moving back over her wet pussy. One hand grips the inside of her thighs, while the other spreads her lips, my thumb pressing against her clit.

Her hand moves from behind her, grabbing and kneading her tit then rolling her nipple between her fingers. Lifting my thumb, my tongue swirls over her swollen clit before I cover her with my mouth sucking and licking as if she is my last meal. Her hips buck forward, her moans filling the room.

Pushing two fingers into her soaked pussy, my tongue is

slow as I move my head from side to side, pushing deeper into her.

"You eat pussy so good," she sobs, her fingers twisting her nipple harder and I smile against her. My fingers pump in and out of her tight little cunt and I watch, my thumb brushing up and over her clit before I delve back in, sucking her swollen nub into my mouth.

"Watch me, you little slut. Watch me eat your cunt," I groan, my cock restrained against the tightness of my trousers.

She does as she's asked, propping herself on her elbows and watching me.

"Fuck," her legs shake as her pussy clenches around me. I look up at her, teasing a finger at her tight little asshole. She doesn't show any sign of not wanting it, so I edge just the tip in and her head falls back.

"You like that baby? You like feeling full," I mutter, lifting my lips from her perfect pussy to ask her.

"Mmhmm," she nods, "yeah."

"I'm going to fuck it after, fill your tight little ass with my cock," I warn her with my dirty talk, her pussy tightening and I fill her ass completely with my finger while fucking her pussy with my two fingers.

"Such a good, fucking girl," I groan, my tongue flicking and swiping over her clit as I devour her, my mouth covering as I suck, lick and eat her little cunt.

"Malachi, I'm getting close," she screams, as I pump into her harder now.

"Touch yourself," I order as her hand skims down her body and rubs over her clit slowly, "faster."

"Oh, oh," she cries, her body shakes as I fuck her pussy and ass hard with my fingers, slipping my little finger in her ass and my thumb into her hot cunt.

"You're so full," I gasp, her wetness running down my fingers, squelching as I finger her.

"I'm going to come, oh fuck," she chokes, her body lurching forward as she comes, squirting. My eyes widen in delight, my mouth over her as I drink her down, making sure not to waste a single drop.

"Oh my god," she pants, as she sits up, her cheeks red and flustered.

"What baby?" I ask, my arms wrapping around her back.

"I squirted," she says bluntly.

"You did, and it was so fucking hot," I kiss the inside of her thighs, "I want to make you do it again," and she blushes. "I'm tense baby, I need to use you, I need to find my release," I kiss her again.

"Then use me baby, I'm yours."

CHAPTER ELEVEN
RYKER

I'VE HAD the day from hell; scrap that, I've had the week from hell. Willow has been working overtime and Malachi has had shit from the poisonous witch. We both need release and the one we use, hasn't been available.

Until tonight.

She's mine and mine only, I'll share tomorrow but tonight, I need just her.

I told her to dress in crotch-less panties and suspenders with nothing else on. I wanted her hair braided and away from her face and I asked her to meet me in the snooker room.

I shower and get changed into shorts before making my way downstairs to see Willow standing by the snooker table.

"Hello Princess," my voice rasps as I take in her appearance. Her full tits on show, her pink nipples hard. Her bare pussy on show through her black lacy crotch-less panties.

"You look beautiful," I admire her as I step closer.

"I feel beautiful," she admits.

"Good, so you should," I kiss her lips, my hands roaming down her body. My hand slips under her, pushing a finger into her soaked pussy.

"Always so ready," I praise, pumping a finger in and out of her, "I'm going to be rough okay, I don't want to hear a peep out of you. You call out 'red' if you can't take it, but I need to fuck. Hard."

She nods, her eyes fluttering shut as I pump in and out.

"Do you understand, Willow?"

"Yes," she pants.

"Good," I tap my finger that is covered in her arousal between her thighs and she widens her stance. Hitting her clit hard, the slap echoes around the room. "Did you like that, you little cock tease?" I taunt, nipping along her jaw line.

"Yes," she whispers as I slap her again.

"Good," I groan pushing two fingers inside of her, pumping faster. "Just working you up, don't you dare fucking come."

She shakes her head from side to side as my free hand grabs and clutches her cheeks.

"You're not going to come until I tell you, are you little girl?" I whisper into the shell of her ear, knowing full well it turns her on. I'm not an arsehole, of course I'll let her come, but I want her to think she isn't allowed to. I want to push her.

"No," she whispers as my thumb rubs her clit.

"Bend over the snooker table," I push her away and she does as I ask, bending over.

"Arms behind your back," I order, stepping behind her and tying her wrists with black ribbon.

I spread her legs wider, two fingers swirling at her opening. Grabbing one of her thighs, I push her leg up on the table, giving me a better view and better access to her glistening cunt. Stepping out of my shorts, I press the tip of my cock in her opening, edging into her before pulling out and rubbing my lubricated cock at her ass. I do it again, coating myself in her arousal and pressing the tip of my cock into her ass.

"I'm going to fuck your ass," I pant, biting my bottom lip and pushing my cock inside of her. She cries out.

"Shh, quiet," I remind her, tugging on her braid as I still for a moment. Pulling out slowly and holding the head of my cock at her opening I slam back into her. This time she doesn't make a sound.

"Good girl," I praise her, skimming my hand down the side of her body and slapping her ass cheek hard. Gripping onto her hips, I drive forward, slamming my hips as my cock fills her.

"You're doing so well," my voice is soft as I swirl a finger at her opening, "do you want more? Do you want my fingers too Princess?" I ask, not stopping with my relentless pounds.

She moans, nodding as hot tears fill her eyes.

"Don't come," I tease, smirking to myself as I push three fingers into her tight little pussy.

"Such a pretty girl, look at you filled with me," I groan, my other hand gripping her peachy ass, pushing into it as I ride her.

"You're getting close, I can feel you tightening around me," I rasp. "Don't. Fucking. Come." I grit between thrusts, the sound of my skin hitting hers filling the room.

I want to force an orgasm out of her, even though I've told her to stop I want her to come so fucking hard because she is enjoying it.

"God, you feel so good," my head tips back as a shiver

dances up my spine, "I wish you could see me, see how your ass is being filled," I reach for my phone, opening up the camera and pushing record. "Let me film you baby, let me film me fucking your ass so you can watch it and see how much of a good girl you're being." I stop, throwing the phone down in front of her as I still, leaning across I press play.

"Watch Princess, see how you've stretched around me," my jaw clenches, "me and Malachi are both going to fuck your tight little cunt, or maybe I'll fuck your ass again." I smile, pulling my fingers from her and focus on just fucking her. "You're so fucking wet, my little whore," I degrade her, not to be nasty but because she likes it.

"I used to see how you pranced around in your skimpy little clothes, your full fucking tits spilling out of your top and your hard nipples straining against the thin material. We both saw, we both knew what you were doing. You wanted to be used by us, to be fucked by older men who knew how to work your body." I continue, pushing four fingers into her cunt and pull to the tip of her ass, before pushing into her. "You're a little slut, and little sluts get punished which is what is happening now."

I look at her, her eyes rolling in the back of her head.

"You like being used, don't you Willow?" I ask her, "You like being used like the little cock teasing slut that you are." And she comes, hard, hot tears rolling down her cheeks as I fuck her hard, pound after pound into her.

"Oh dear, you naughty little girl, I told you not to come."

I slap her ass cheek hard, the sound of the snap echoing. I pull out of her sudden and fast as her cum trickles down her legs. I turn, reaching for a snooker cue and twist it round in my hands so the thicker end is in my grasp.

"Shall we try that again?" I ask, stepping behind her and pushing the end of the cue into her, just past the tip and she gasps, eyes wide at the coolness of the wood as I push it deeper into her, fucking her slowly.

"Ryker," she sobs, but I don't stop. My eyes fall as I watch the long cue slip in and out of her cunt with ease.

"Look how fucking wet you are, are you still horny Willow?" I ask, pushing the cue a little deeper and feeling the resistance.

"Will you let me fuck your ass again until I come? Then I am going to film when my cum runs out of your ass and push it into your tight little pussy," I groan, twisting and slipping the cue in and out. "Answer me, Princess."

"Yes," she rasps, "yes."

Slipping the cue from her, I drop it to the floor and dip my fingers inside of her, swirling her come at her ass before pushing into her, filling her to the hilt.

This time I don't go gentle.

I fuck her hard and raw, taking everything I can from her.

I still, grabbing my phone and opening the camera and film my cock slipping in and out with ease, my orgasm building.

"Fuck, I'm going to come," I grit as my orgasm explodes through me, I pull out and film as my cum leaks and drips out of her ass, and as promised, I push it inside her cunt.

CHAPTER TWELVE
WILLOW

It's been a year since my mum walked out. A year of loving these two beautiful men. A year of being worshipped and I am so glad I am here with them.

As I wait for them to get back from the gym, I sit waiting, naked on the bed.

Tonight, I get them both.

I don't take them like this too often, if you know what I'm saying. Last time I did, I had both of their cocks inside my pussy, stretching me and filling me to the hilt. Moans were floating around the room, we were all too lost in the moment to notice that my mum walked in, and she stood watching as her daughter got fucked by her ex-husband—her daughter's ex-stepdad—and his best friend. She ran for the hills, and we have never seen her since.

"There's our girl," Malachi's voice pulls me from my thoughts as he strips down, Ryker behind him.

"Hello Princess," Ryker smiles, undressing himself.

Malachi climbs behind me, lifting me up and lowering me onto his already hard cock as Ryker climbs between his thighs and lines his cock at my opening, filling me in one swift move as they're cocks rub together as they fuck me.

Malachi's hand rests on my small bump, Ryker kissing me as we spend the evening lost in each other.

They are my forever.

My husbands.

The three of us, soon to be four, living our happily ever after.

The End

ACKNOWLEDGEMENTS

Dan. My best friend. My husband. My world. Thank you for pushing me to start this crazy journey. I love you to the moon and back.

Thanks firstly to Robyn, for keeping me in check and always being there when I needed you.

My girls, our little group. Thank you for the constant support and love you give me. I am so grateful to have you in my life and being with me on this crazy author journey.

My BETA's and friends, Sophie and Harriet. Thank you for being honest and loving my characters as much as I do.

Leanne, thank you for always being here for me. You're a friend for life.

Lea Joan, thank you once again for squeezing this in last minute. You have always been by my side in my author journey and I am so grateful that I get to work with you.

And lastly, my readers... without you, none of this would have been possible.
    My loyal fans, I owe it all to you.

WANTING KNOX

PROLOGUE
KNOX

I ALWAYS KNEW my best friend's kid sister was off limits.

Completely off limits.

But that didn't stop me watching her as she grew. I was a lot older than her, but as soon as she was *legal,* I couldn't get her off my mind. I knew it was wrong, but forbidden fruit always tastes the best, right?

I had grown up with her brother, Cooper. We went to school together and just sailed through life until we both got scouted and put into a scholarship, and once that was done, we both joined Seattle Steels and haven't looked back since. Cooper and his family moved out to Seattle when we got on the team whereas my family stayed back in Boston. It's only me and my parents. Only child. They wanted to come, but I told them to stay behind. They weren't in the best of health; they lived close to my mom's sister, and she helps out a lot. Even more so now I'm not there.

CHAPTER ONE
KNOX

We had a game this afternoon, and my head was all over the place. We were playing against our rival team. Nashville Nemesis. They were dirty, rough, and wouldn't stop until they had us down on points, but we were dirtier, rougher and we won't stop until the game is ours. Music thrums through my ears as I scroll through my social feed, stopping when I see her. *Tate.*

Her long, blonde curls tumble down around her. The emerald in her eyes so bright as they pierce through mine. My heart drums under my white tee, I have my grey sweatshirt hood pulled over my head. I sigh, scrolling by as I feel a slap round the back of my head. I jump and look over my shoulder to see Cooper.

"What are you doing?" he asks, slumping down next to me on the sofa, as I tug my earphone out.

"Just having some downtime," my eyes lift to the clock, a smirk pulling at my lips.

"You ready for the game?" Cooper asks, twisting the lid of his drink and taking a mouthful.

"Ready as I can be." I turn to look at him, my cocky

smile replacing the smirk. "The question is Cooper, are you?"

"So ready," he leans forward, rubbing his hands together.

"Your family coming to watch?" I try to hide the excitement creeping up my throat.

"Yeah of course, home game to us isn't it," he nudges into me, "fuck, I am pumped."

"You seem it," I agree, because he does. His energy is electrifying, if he could, he would be bouncing off the fucking walls. He pushes up, running behind me and rubbing my shoulders.

"Get hyped with me man, we're going to smash the Nashville Nemesis."

"I know mate, I know," I chuckle, darting forward to stand, breaking his hands off me.

"Let's go and see the rest of the team, it's game time baby." Cooper winks at me, slapping me on the back as he turns to walk out the lounge. I should be excited for the game, but I'm not. I'm more excited about seeing Tate standing behind the glass, in the front row watching me. Well, watching her brother, but I can pretend she is looking at me.

I snort a laugh, shaking my head from side to side and follow Cooper out of the room.

When did I become *this* dude?

CHAPTER TWO
TATE

Brushing my hair out of its tight ringlets and setting my middle parting, I smile at my reflection. Wearing my grey and silver Seattle Steels jersey with my brother's number on the back, but all I want is to be wearing Knox's. All I want is *Knox*.

But it'll never happen.

He is far *too* old for me.

This is what happens when your parents have you in their forties and the age gap between you and your brother is ten years.

I'm just a *kid* to Knox. It doesn't matter how much I try and make him look at me, to make him *see* me and show him that I am grown. I'm not a little girl anymore. Sighing, I slip my gold hoops through my ears and fiddle with the thin gold chain that hangs round my neck, dangling a simple T.

"Are you ready?" my mom calls up the stairs.

"Yup, just getting my shoes on!" I shout back. Cooper's jersey swamps me and fits more like a dress than a top. I finish off my look with wide legged, light denim jeans and slip my feet into my black and white dunks.

I give myself a quick spray of my perfume then pose in the floor length mirror and lift my phone out to take a photo. I turn to the side, bending and lifting one of my legs and tipping my head back slightly as I smile and take the photo. I smirk at it, posting it straight onto my grid, then onto my stories. Knox always watches my stories but will never like the post so now I only post on my stories for him.

"Tate!" my mom bellows and I rush out my bedroom, running down the stairs.

"Sorry," I say sweetly and angelic.

"It's okay, I just want to see your brother before the game starts," she says, pride etched all over her face, her eyes glistening with happiness.

My dad appears, placing his hands on my mom's shoulders as he kisses her on the cheek. They're both wearing Seattle Steels jerseys too, but my dad has Knox's number on the back, and I have never been as envious of a number ten as I am now. We will always be my brother and Knox's biggest supporters, seeing as Knox only has us that go to his games due to his parent's ill health.

My Instagram app begins to notify me of likes and comments, and I smile. Slipping into the back of our SUV, I plug my seat belt across and open my app.

The same old comments.

Go Alder!

Go Steels!

You look beautiful.

Pretty.

Come on Steels!

But I'm not interested in that, I hover over my story and

swipe up to see that Knox has seen it and my heart drums in my chest. The smile grows on my face as we pull off the drive and onto the road.

Just under an hour till I get to see him.

CHAPTER THREE
KNOX

PACING UP and down the locker room, nerves wrack me, but it's not because of the game. No, these games don't worry me. It's because of *her*.

The constant reminder of her. She makes my heart thump, my cock hard and my mind dirty. The things I want to do to her should be considered a sin. Rage soon consumes me when I think about the guys she has been with before, anger seeps through my pores causing me to stand still in my tracks, my nostrils flare, my jaw clenched and tight as my fists ball at my side.

"You okay?" Cooper sneaks up beside me, his hand on my shoulder and I shrug him off.

"Yeah, yeah, I'm fine." I snap, stepping away from him as I run my hand over my face.

"What's got you like this?" Cooper asks me, not getting the hint that I need a minute. "Is it the game? Cos bro, you know we're going to kill them." He grabs me, pressing his forehead to mine. "We're the best defence players in the league, you know we aren't going to let their puck slip past us," he presses his head harder onto mine. "Get your head in the game Knox, we can't lose this..." he pauses, stepping back, "we're not going to lose this are we?"

I shake my head from side to side, "No, of course not." Rolling my shoulders back, I stand taller. "It's fine, just had a moment," I swallow the large lump that bobs in my throat.

Cooper gives a knowing nod towards me before he turns and hypes the rest of the team up, then he bounds over to Roach, our goalie. I smirk, as the room erupts into shouting and cheers.

Nothing could beat the pre-game excitement, it's the best. We all get riled up ready to smash the opposing team into the boards. We play dirty, but it's why we're the best.

Half an hour passes and the room is still a buzz with chanting and chatting between friends, I look between my *team* and smile with pride. I couldn't have chosen a better team to play for. We are united, our bonds infinite and nothing could make me walk away from them.

Coach Greaves walks in, shouting and clapping his hands together to silence us and suddenly the room is deadly silent.

"Boys, this is a big game. Don't get focused on smashing them into the boards, you need to focus on winning." His eyes scan the room as he looks at Justin, he is our centre player and likes to cause a stir whilst on the ice. He has no fear, he is reckless. "Play through them, focus on the endgame. We don't want a loss on our streak, we haven't come this far to be beaten by the Nashville Nemesis just because you all want a ruck on the ice. Keep ya head in the game, not anywhere else," his eyes scan the room making eye contact which each of us and for some reason it feels like they linger on mine a little longer than anyone else's.

We all nod and cheer as we finish getting our gear on. I

have my helmet in my hand, holding it tightly as my mouth guard rests between my fingers while we wait to walk out to the player's bench. Nerves crackle through me, the atmosphere is amazing as always as we see a flood of grey jerseys behind the boards. My eyes seek out only her, but I don't see her. Disappointment blankets over me as we take our seats on the bench, when suddenly, I feel her presence.

Turning slowly, Mauve runs for me, giving me a big hug and a kiss on the cheek before stepping back to hug and kiss Cooper. Rich swoops in, shaking my hand firmly and gives me a pat on the back.

"Go get them," he laughs, pulling me in for an excited hug before he moves to Cooper.

That's when I see her. My eyes widen as I drink her in. She dons her usual loose curled hair, her emerald eyes shining under the bright lights. Her cheeks are slightly pink, crimson even. *Is she blushing?* I shake the thought from my head, ignoring myself. Don't be so stupid.

Fuck, she looks good in that jersey, but I want her in *mine*, because number ten will never look as good as it does on her. My lucky number on her, my forbidden fruit.

"Hey," she steps towards me slowly and I seem to have lost the ability to speak, my tongue suddenly too big for my mouth. So what do I do? I smile.

"Ready for the game?" she takes another step, one more and she'll be pressed against me.

I nod, finally managing to get a word out. "Yeah."

"Good, I'll be screaming your name from where I'm standing..." she trails off, her eyes fluttering shut for a moment before they connect with mine and she throws a wink my way.

"Is that so?" My nostrils flare, my chest pushing out

slightly and all I can imagine is her on her back as I ride her whilst she is screaming my name.

"Yeah, it is," her fingers reach for my chest, hovering before finally letting them spread across my jock protector, feeling my neck guard she drums her fingers against it. "It's all I have wanted, to feel what it would be like for your name to repeat on my tongue until my voice is hoarse and my throat is sore from *screaming*."

I swallow. Is she *flirting* with me? This is new.

"You don't know what you're doing to me cub."

"Then show me," she whispers, lifting her fingers from my chest and I instantly miss it.

"Tate..."

"Knox..." she mimics me, but her tone is low, teasing and fucking sensual and all I can think about is sinking my heavy, thick cock into her, hard and fast, pounding into her in punishing thrusts.

She steps back, her eyes skimming down my body before lifting to my eyes. "Good luck, baby," she says softly so only my ears hear it.

"Are you going to be my good luck charm, tater tot?" I smirk, and she leans forward swatting me on the arm.

"I hope so, Henderson," she licks her lips as she steps further back, her mom and dad appearing at her side.

"Good luck, we will be cheering you all on, go Steels!" Rich shouts as the crowd begins to drum up the noise.

I give him a little salute off my head with my finger, they turn and my eyes are pinned to her, her eyes find mine one last time as she looks over her shoulder at me. My heart thrums against my chest, my stomach flipping and I feel like I am free falling until Cooper pulls me round to face him.

"It's game time, baby."

We all move together, our sticks all touching as the coach goes through the game plan once more, but my mind is too full of Tate.

Maybe I have read it all wrong, maybe she does want me as much as I want her.

CHAPTER FOUR
TATE

Nerves rip through me as I watch Knox fight off the Nashvilles, they're playing rough, but Justin makes it his goal to do whatever he needs to stop them getting in our end. I watch as Knox darts forward as Jenkins from Nemesis slips past Justin and knocks into Cooper, flooring him. Knox helps him up and as soon as Cooper is on his feet, Jenkins gets up in Cooper's face, pushing him into the boards and I feel my heart drop from my chest.

I know exactly where this is going as soon as Cooper's eyes seek out mine, but then Knox's slice over to me and that hurts the most. I feel the tears prick in my eyes at the shame that is colouring my skin; I never wanted this to get out. It was just a mistake. A dirty secret that was meant to be buried.

But secrets never stay buried.

KNOX

"What the fuck?!" I scream at Jenkins who grins down at Cooper where he has just floored him. The ref's whistle is screaming, the crowd is in uproar and our teammates are chest to chest with the Nashvilles.

Reaching down, I pull Coop up to his feet, patting him on the back.

"What is your problem you little prick?" Coop shoves Jenkins who darts forward, pushing Coop into the boards.

I rush over to where Cooper is pinned when I hear Tate's name leave the cunt's lips. I reach them, sliding between them and knocking Jenkins over and smirk as he crashes into the ice. Every other noise has drowned out around us and all I can hear is the blood thumping in my ears.

"What did you just say?" I grin down at him, and it takes everything in me not to lift my skate and *accidentally* slice through his fingers. Cooper is beside me as one of Jenkins' teammates helps him up and he is soon back in Cooper's face.

"Your sister, Tate. She is quite the good little *slut*, honestly, I never expected her to be as good of a fuck as she was," he rolls his eyes, smirking and shaking his head as if he is replaying a memory only he knows. I turn to face Cooper, but his eyes are on Tate's and when I follow his gaze we can tell by the tears in her eyes that Jenkins isn't lying.

I feel the air leave my lungs and the rage consumes me, but Cooper beats me to it, shoving into Jenkins, knocking him off his balance and swiping his feet away with his stick.

"Don't ever speak my sister's name and slut in the same sentence; better yet, never fucking mention my sister's name you worthless piece of shit." Cooper spits on him, sneakily hitting him with the end of his stick and skating off to the player's bench. I lean down, gripping him by his shitty jock protector, lifting him off the ice slightly.

"Don't ever fucking look in her direction, you are to never look at her, don't even fucking breathe near her, do you understand me?"

I can hear the commotion of the ref beside me, the coach is screaming my name, but I turn my face up to look at Tate who has tears rolling down her pretty little face.

"Don't think she is into old men," Jenkins jibes me and I clench my jaw.

"You think we're surprised by your little admission? She told me she slept with a weasel with a micro dick, I just didn't know she was talking about you Jenkins, but now we have confirmation." I drop him onto the ice, his helmet hitting the hard, cold surface and causing an echo. "Now, stop being a little cunt and fuck off," I grit my teeth, my jaw clenched as I join Cooper on the player's bench.

I knew we were off, no point causing a commotion. Jenkins was pulled off too and disappeared onto his bench.

I was raging, I didn't give a shit about the game now. My eyes darkened, my jaw tight as I sat and replayed Jenkins words over and over in my head.

CHAPTER FIVE
KNOX

THE LOCKER ROOM was finally empty. We won 7-2 and the guys were buzzing, even Cooper. His anger soon left as excitement coursed through him, but me? I just couldn't shake my rage. Sitting on the bench, my back against the wall and my head tilted back, I just sat in the silence. I had showered and had only managed to get my sweatpants on.

I had no idea how long I had been sitting there alone when I heard the locker room door squeak, I didn't even have it in me to turn my head to see who it was. I wasn't interested.

Soft footsteps slowly approach, and I know who it was instantly, but I still refuse to look at her. I am too angry.

"Knox," her voice is small as she stands in front of me, her head dipping down as she looks at her feet.

I finally give in to the pull, my eyes raking up her body as I focus on her beautiful green eyes.

"I'm..." she stammers, knotting her fingers in front of her.

"Tate..." I breathe out, puffing my cheeks out, and I can't stop the pull on my lips as I smirk at her. She doesn't say anything. "Why Jenkins? Do you like him?" I ask, leaning forward on the bench and pushing my hands under her jersey, hooking my fingers in the loops of her jeans, tugging her so she is close to me.

"Not particularly."

Her answer annoys me even more. I close my eyes for a moment and inhale deeply, I'm trying so hard to simmer the rage that is burning through my veins.

"You're infuriating me."

"Why is that? Do you hate the fact that someone has fucked me?" she sticks her bottom lip out before pouting.

She drives me wild. Insane. Makes me completely feral. I lose all composure that I once had, tugging her even closer so she is between my parted legs.

"I *hate* the fact that you've been with anyone but me," my eyes pin to hers, her eyes volley back and forth between mine, her perfect, plump lips part as she chokes on her inhale.

"But you have never shown any interest, I couldn't just sit and wait and hope that one day you'd see me."

"I've always seen you, but I've never been able to go there with you."

"What because you're older than me?" her brows furrow and she tries to pull back but I don't let her.

"No, because you're my best friend's *kid* sister."

"Too bad for you then, maybe I'll go and find Jenkins..." she places her hands over mine and pushes them off her body before she turns to walk away, but something inside me snaps. I lurch forward, grabbing her around the waist and pulling her into me, her back hitting my front.

"Don't you fucking dare," I growl against the shell of her ear, turning her to face me. She goes to speak, but she doesn't get a chance.

I cup her face, her face tilting up to look at me and I slam my lips against hers. Even kissing her isn't calming the anger that is brewing deep inside of me. My kiss is hard, my tongue hungry as it swipes and glides against hers. I want to make her forget anyone who has had her before me. Letting my hands fall from her face, I glide them down her petite frame and cup under her ass, lifting her up effortlessly and a small, delicious squeal leaves her.

"You sure about this?" I groan as I break away from the kiss, my skin erupting in goosebumps as her nails drag softly against my skin.

"Never been surer of something in my life," she whispers, her lips hovering over mine as she grabs the hem of her jersey, "but I need to get this off." I nod. It's bad enough I'm about to fuck my best friend's sister, but I don't want to fuck her with his number on her back.

She lifts the jersey over her head, discarding it to the floor and I dive forward, my lips on her neck as I lick, kiss and suck on her soft skin. Her heartbeat thumps underneath my lips at a steady beat. Her hands are in my hair, pulling my lips from her skin so she can sink her lips over mine in a slow, torturous kiss before she pulls on my bottom lip with her teeth.

I walk her towards the locker, her back hitting the cool metal. I let her down gently, falling to my knees as I unfasten the button of her jeans and tug them down her legs. Her hands find my broad shoulders as she balances herself, removing one foot at a time. I throw them on the bench before my eyes glide up her body, taking every inch of her in until my eyes finally land on hers.

Her long blonde hair frames her face, her eyes fluttering as she blinks, her chest rising and falling fast.

Pushing my lips against her inner thigh, I trail soft kisses against her hot skin.

"Tell me," I whisper, looking up at her through my lashes, "did he taste you?"

She shakes her head, shallow pants leaving her.

"Good," I groan, lifting my lips and pressing them on her other thigh, hooking my long finger in the side of her scrap of material and pull it to the side, exposing her bare pussy. Sinking my teeth into my bottom lip, I fall back on my knees as I reach for her with my other hand and push her lips apart, sucking in a breath through my teeth.

"Look at your pretty little pussy glistening."

"Knox," she whispers, as I lift her leg and place it over my shoulder, then tap her inner thigh of her left leg for her to spread out a little.

"Remember what you said before the game?" I let my eyes find hers.

She doesn't speak, just nibbles her bottom lip, her hands kneading her tits.

"You said you were going to be screaming my name. Now baby, I want you to show me how good my name sounds coming off your tongue whilst you cum on mine."

"Fuck," she whispers, as I swipe my tongue through her parted lips, flicking it against her clit then gliding it down to her opening, swirling and teasing before I'm back on her clit, sucking and nibbling. My fingers dig into her sensitive skin, my spare hand skimming up to her bare stomach and holding her in place to stop her wriggling.

I have dreamt of eating her pussy, dreamt of her beautiful moans filling my ears as I send her to new realms of pleasure. And here I am, living my dream as I fucking devour her. I'm messy, not stopping until I know she is coming all over my face. I bury my tongue deeper, trailing my hand to her other thigh and lift it over my left shoulder, then grip to her waist as I hold her where I want her.

Slowly grazing my fingers under her ass, I let them trail down behind her and tease at her opening, edging the tip of two fingers into her soaked pussy which causes her hips to buck forward, coating me in her arousal as my tongue laps across her sensitive clit.

"Oh, Knox," she pants, her fingers find my hair as she tugs at the root, pushing me deeper into her cunt.

Edging a little further into her, I curl my fingers as I rub her g-spot then slowly begin pumping in and out of her, matching the strokes of my tongue against her clit.

"Please Knox, I need more," she begs, and I lift my mouth from her, so I can look at her, my fingers still fucking her.

"Then come," I smirk, throwing a wink at her as I lurch forward and sink my tongue between her lips, sucking on her clit.

I tease her with a third fingertip causing Tate to mewl in appreciation as I slip it into her, fucking her with three of my fingers now. Her tight little cunt constricts around my fingers, her pelvis tilting up slightly, giving me better access.

"Such a greedy girl," I whisper between my tongue strokes.

"Knox," she moans, and I smirk against her, tilting my head to the side slightly and press my tongue flat against her clit.

"Shit," she cries.

I hear a bang and I'm assuming it's the back of her head hitting the lockers.

"Are you going to come for me pretty girl?" my fingers fuck her faster, harder.

"Yes, so fucking hard," she cries, her fingers knot in my hair but I ignore the burn that she is causing where she is pulling at the root so hard. My erection is bulging and I felt my own orgasm growing at how she makes me feel, how she looks and sounds as I pleasure her.

Her pussy clenches tightly as she grinds down on my fingers, her hips rocking back and forth slowly and I feel her lose control.

She screams my name, the pleasure that laces her voice turning me on. I slide my tongue to her opening, lapping up her cum as the wetness coats my fingers, the most delicious sound echoing round the empty locker room. I pull away from her, watching as my fingers continue to fuck her, her pretty little pussy stretched and for a moment I'm worried she won't be able to take all of me, but I'll make it fit. Her arousal coats my hand, a few drips running down my wrist and I smirk up at her.

"Enjoying this, baby?" I ask in a raspy tone as I slowly lift her legs down and I smirk as they tremble in my grip. I don't stop fucking her, I know she is going to be over sensitive now, but she looks too fucking hot with my fingers buried deep in her wet, little cunt.

She nods slowly, her eyes hazy from the orgasm that ripped through her. She reaches between her legs and starts swirling her fingers over her clit.

"You're such a turn on," I rasp, my eyes focused on her pussy but just as she gets into it, she stops, reaching for my hand and slipping my fingers from her pussy. She lifts them to her lips and sucks the three of them clean whilst her eyes stay pinned on mine. "Oh fuck," I moan as pleasure ripples through me.

She grabs my chin, her fingers tight as she grips, and

pulls me to my feet. I tower over her, causing her hand to drop.

"Now it's my turn," her voice silkily dances over my skin as her fingers run under the waistband of my sweatpants, then hungrily tugs them down my thick, toned thighs.

Her eyes widen, glazing with delight as she looks from my cock to my face, and she smiles.

"I want you to take all of me," I grip a fistful of her hair, tipping her head back so she has no option now but to look at me. "Do you understand? I want your greedy little mouth to take every, single, inch of me."

She nods eagerly, licking her lips.

"You're such a good girl," I croon, stepping forwards as I pull her towards me. Her hands wrap around my girthy length as she purses her lips at my tip. Her tongue swipes across, licking the precum away then hollowing her cheeks as she takes me to the back of her throat. Her body lurches forward as she gags, slipping me from her mouth. "Take it slow, princess..."

"Don't princess me, I'm no princess." She winks, readjusting herself on her knees as her hand glides up and down my hard cock. "I want to be your *slut*."

I choke on my own breath as she pushes her hot, wet mouth down my cock, stilling when she gets to the base and this time, she doesn't gag.

"Shit," I suck in a harsh breath, and she slips me in and out of her mouth then twirls her tongue at my tip and just when I think she is about to swallow me whole, she flattens her tongue and runs it down the underside of my cock.

"Tate," I grit out, my head tipping back as I grab a bigger fistful of her hair, her hot mouth slipping down my cock. "I'm going to explode," I moan, moving her head up and down, her teeth gently grazing along the sensitive skin.

She pulls me from her mouth, then spits on me.

"Tate, fuck."

Rubbing her thumb over the tip of my dick, my balls tighten as the rest of my skin tingles.

"Open your fucking mouth, *slut*." The word feels disgusting on my tongue, but it brings out the animal inside of her.

She does as I say, sitting on her knees, her emerald eyes on me as she sits, waiting with her mouth open. I fist myself, keeping my eyes locked on her.

"Fuck, you look so fucking pretty on your knees like the good girl you are."

My jaw clenches, my head falling forward as pleasure consumes me. She kneels up, taking me in her mouth as I wrap my hand around the back of her head, holding her there as I fuck her mouth. Saliva runs down her chin, her moans pushing me to continue.

"Tate, I'm going to come," I grit, my hips thrusting fast, my cock slipping in and out of her mouth sloppily.

My ears ring, my head spins and my eyes roll in the back of my head as she sucks the life from me, I lurch forward spurting hot cum down the back of her throat.

"Fuck!" I roar, as a shiver blankets me causing me to shudder.

She falls back, wiping the corner of her mouth before standing.

"You are something else," I smile through a mumble, pulling her towards me as I wrap my arms around her. We just stand for a while, completely forgetting where we are, just lost in this moment.

CHAPTER SIX
TATE

Knox sits across the street, under the shadows of the streetlamps. I walk up the front path to our large stately home and as I get to the front door, I stop in my tracks and look over my shoulder, he wouldn't be able to see but I gave him a smile before quietly opening the front door. Stepping inside, I let out a sigh of relief. I turn and jump in my skin as I see Cooper standing with his arms crossed against his broad chest.

"Where have you been? Mom said you were meeting someone."

"Well then you know where I was," I say sarcastically.

"It's dark, I don't like you being out when it's dark." Cooper doesn't budge so I walk round him. Rolling my eyes, I shake my head from side to side.

"I'm twenty, I'm not a kid, why does everyone see me as this innocent, fragile child!?" I snap.

"Woah," Cooper is hot on my tail, grabbing me by the arm and spinning me round to face him. His eyes are searching my face for something, anything, to give him a hint at my random outburst.

"Has something happened?" his condescending tone is now replaced with concern.

"No, I'm fine," I tug my arm out of his grip and turn for the stairs. I baffled myself at my outburst, but maybe it was just the realisation that Knox sees me as his best friend's kid sister.

I blow out a sigh, stepping into my room and closing the door behind me. Kicking my sneakers off, I head for my bathroom, stripping my clothes from my sticky body.

This afternoon was one of the best in my life, sad, but it's true. Knox was a dream come true and I just hope and pray he doesn't regret me. I have loved Knox for as long as I could remember, even down to the silly schoolgirl crush. It was always Knox.

Stepping under the hot water, I wash the day from me. Lathering my skin in a peach body wash. I somehow have his scent all over me and it mixes with the peach scent filling my senses with him. He is all I can think about as I run my fingers over my pebbled skin slowly, gliding them across my areola before skimming them ever so softly over my hardened nipples. My eyes flutter shut, my head falling back as I turn the pressure of the hot shower water up, the droplets hitting my skin harder now which only makes my skin more sensitive.

The breath I inhale shakes as I continue my teasing trail down my pebbled skin, the whole time imagining what Knox would be doing if he were here. *His hard body pressed up behind me, his lips kissing the shell of my ear before letting them drop to my neck, my collar bone, across my shoulder whilst his hand skims down my wet body and curves between my legs.* Widening my stance, my fingers slip between my lips, rubbing over my swollen clit. My pussy clenches as I roll my hardened nipple between my fingers, imagining the whole time it was Knox's hot, wet mouth.

My body stiffens as I rub my clit harder, gliding my fingers through my lips and teasing at my soaked opening, pushing my finger deep inside me which causes my orgasm to rip through me. Crying out choked moans as the hot water cascades down over me, my body trembles and my legs buckle. I reach out, gripping onto the shower rail to steady myself.

I wait a while before I open my eyes, I let my body ride its orgasm and come down from its almighty high slowly.

The following weekend rolls around and I'm miserable. I haven't heard from Knox, he has even stopped watching my stories. Rage bubbles inside of me but my heart aches. I lay on my bed, music playing as my eyes fix on the ceiling as I play all different scenarios out in my head as to why he hasn't called.

I twist my head to face my bedroom door as I hear Cooper calls out that he is home. I roll up, resting my upper half on my elbows, my eyes fixated on the small gap between my door and its frame.

I hear a low rumbling laugh and I know it's Knox. I jump up, looking at the mess that I am in the mirror and run my fingers through my tight curls before pinching my cheeks to get a little colour in them. I hate that Cooper still lives at home, that means Knox comes round whenever he feels like it. If Cooper just flew the nest, I wouldn't have to worry about shit like this.

Rushing around, I spray my perfume and jump back on my bed as I hear their voices disappear down the hallway.

Relief swarms me as I sit on my bed, flicking my tele on and letting *Friends* play whilst my heart drums in my chest. Nerves slowly crackle to rage. I lean forward, grabbing my phone and slipping my yoga pants down to kick them off my ankles. Positioning my legs, I slip my hand down the front of my red, lace g-string and snap a picture. I scroll through my contacts and click on Knox's name, attach the photo and type a message.

> Can't wait to see you xo.

My heart is racing in my chest and I click send on the message, I smirk to myself when I hear a ding of a phone, watching my screen to watch it go from unread to read. I begin to type again.

> Oopsie, that wasn't meant for you. It was for Jenkins.

My smile grows wider, my erratic heartbeat growing wilder.

Another ding, and another two ticks to show it's been read. I giggle to myself, dropping my phone into my top drawer before slipping on my yoga pants. I skip out my bedroom, practically running down the stairs. I twirl at the bottom, holding onto the stair post, swinging round it and walking down the long hallway.

"What's with your mood suddenly?" Cooper asks Knox and I smirk as I step into the kitchen. Cooper turns to look at me and smiles before turning his back to me, but Knox is still facing me.

I ignore Knox's heated stare that is burning into my back as I reach up, purposely over reaching so my crop top lifts, and he gets just the right amount of under boob on show.

"I am parched," I mumble, grabbing my glass and spinning round, "drink?"

"Yeah, I'll have a water please. Knox?" Cooper asks and I stand with a smug smile on my face as Knox's hooded eyes glare in my direction but his fingers dance over his phone screen.

"Who you texting?" I ask, stepping closer to them but his brows pinch when he realises I don't have my phone on me.

I shrug my shoulders up and reach for another glass for Cooper. Turning the lever for the faucet I place the cups under the stream one at a time.

I pace over to Cooper and Knox who are now sitting on the sofa in the kitchen sunroom. I lean across Knox, his scent consuming me as I pass Cooper his drink.

"Thanks Tate," he smiles, taking his glass and taking a mouthful. I slowly stand, my fingers brushing across Knox's thigh as I stand tall. Cooper is too engrossed in his phone to witness my behaviour.

Stepping back I take a mouthful, but *accidentally* miss my mouth so the water runs down my chin and onto my white top.

"Oh shoot," I sigh, bending over and placing my glass on the coffee table that sits in front of Knox. "I'm all *wet*," I shake my head from side to side as I feel my nipples harden against the cold, wet material.

"Fuck's sake Tate, I don't need to see this! Go get changed." Cooper squeezes his eyes shut, clamping his hand over his eyes for good measure.

I smirk, turning to look at Knox and give him a slow, seductive wink as I turn and walk away, rocking my hips from side to side. I risk looking over my shoulder at him to see his eyes fixed to my ass. I slowly run my tongue across my top lip before disappearing.

As soon as I am out of sight, I run down the hallway, stomping up the stairs and into my room. My heart is in my throat, I have no idea why I act that way in front of him but I love it. I love the rush it gave me, it makes me feel brazen. The fire hits my cheeks suddenly, the breath snatched from my lungs.

I place my back against my bedroom door as my heart rate begins to slow. Exhaling deeply, I step forward and walk towards my bedside unit, grabbing my phone.

Smiling when I see the notifications from Knox, I click on the messages and begin to read.

> Jenkins?! Are you fucking winding me up?
>
> Answer your phone, Tate
>
> I am going to fuck you so good you won't remember Jenkins.
>
> Nice show, Tate. Watch your back... you want to play games? I can play them better.
>
> You're such a teasing slut.

Heat swarms between my legs, wetness blossoming at his dirty words. My chest rises as my clit throbs.

I need him, so *so badly*.

Slamming the drawer shut, I lift my wet tee over my head, discarding it before grabbing a sports bra. I need to burn of this tension.

Grabbing my phone and earphones, I escape my room and slip downstairs into the basement gym. I head for the running machine, pushing my earphones in and blasting

Blink 182 – Edging as loud as my phone will allow and ignore the fact that my body is screaming with want and need.

By the time I am finished, I am covered in sweat. Moving to the pull up bar, I reach up and lift myself, crossing my legs at my ankles as I lift myself up and down. I shouldn't be pushing myself, but having him so close is teasing me beyond belief. I could orgasm just looking at him, that's how pent up I am.

My phone buzzes in my pocket and I fall to the mat beneath me, my arms heavy.

Slipping it out I see another message from Knox.

> Where are you? You're not in your room.

I scoff.

> I'm somewhere you're not, obviously.

Slipping my phone back into my pants, I get ready to pull myself up again when it vibrates. Rolling my eyes, I slip it out once more.

> That smart mouth of yours is going to get you into trouble.

I ignore him.

Dropping my phone to the mat, I stretch my arms out before lifting myself back up. Everything in me aches, my body burning and screaming for me to stop but it's not enough to dampen the ache in my stomach and the throbbing in my pussy. I need *more*.

After fifteen more reps, I give in, letting go and flopping down on the mat as my chest rises and falls fast.

I roll onto my front, grabbing my phone and hitting skip on the next song. Opening the camera, I pout, closing my eyes as I take a selfie. The sweat beads on my forehead, my blonde hair wet. Lifting the phone higher so I can get my body in it too. Dropping my arms, I smile as I look at the photo and post it onto my grid, as well as my stories.

I text my friends back that I have ignored all week then scroll social media whilst I let my heart rate slow.

I freeze when I feel hands on my waist, digging their fingers into my skin. Then I feel my earphone being pulled out.

"Found you," he breathes, nipping my earlobe before sucking it into his mouth.

"Bully for you," I moan, a bolt of pleasure zapping through me.

"You're such a little tease, I know what you're doing," he moves back. His large hands squeezing my peachy ass in my yoga pants.

"I'm resting after my work out," I say deadpan.

"You're so cocky," he licks his lips as I look at him over my shoulder, his fingers digging and kneading into me.

"I am so hard for you."

"You better go and sort yourself out then," I smirk, pushing up and out of his hands.

I bend down, grabbing my earphone off the mat before walking out of the gym and not looking back.

Fuck.

CHAPTER SEVEN
TATE

SITTING AT THE DINNER TABLE, I eat small mouthfuls of my food as I listen to my mom and dad talk to Knox. His deep, sultry, silky voice is pushing me closer and closer to exploding. Of course, he decided to sit next to me so every now again he grips my thigh with his hand.

"How are your parents, Knox?" my mom asks as she butters her bread roll.

"They're doing okay, some days are better than others," Knox sighs as he takes a mouthful of mom's brisket. His finger swirls over my jeans in a slow and tortuous manner and all I can think about is how good his touch would feel on my skin.

"I'm glad to hear it, when are you heading back home?" My dad asks.

"Hopefully during the season break, be good to see them. It's been far too long." This time his hand dips between my parted thighs, rubbing me on the seam of my jeans, causing me to fidget on the spot.

Mom and dad nod in agreement, Cooper shuffles in his seat.

"Will you guys be coming to our game in Texas next weekend?" he asks and I am grateful because the sound of Knox's voice is too much.

"That's the plan my boy," my dad booms, smiling. I love how proud he is of my brother, we're all so proud of him.

It has always been his dream to play ice hockey; at least he has a dream. My dream? Having my brother's best friend fuck me raw. I sigh, which causes all eyes to land on mine.

"Everything okay darling?" my mom asks, her brows furrowing, concern etched over her face.

I snap from my hazy thoughts and lift my eyes to meet hers while swallowing the dryness down, willing saliva to coat my tongue.

I nod, "I think I have a migraine coming on, do you mind if I am excused?" I push my chair back. "I'm going to the bathroom to get some Advil."

"Of course," my mom smiles, and I stand quickly, keeping my head down as I walk out of the dining room and into the bathroom down the hall, rushing in and shutting the door behind me. Letting out a deep inhale, I wrap my fingers around the edge of one of the cool basins which sits in the double sink unit, the porcelain cooling my burning skin instantly. I feel like a ticking time bomb, ready to detonate at any second.

Closing my eyes, I let my head fall forward as I enjoy the silence, as I enjoy not having the constant magnetism that is Knox. The tension crackles between us, the gravitational force field that surrounds him when he is near is enough to set off the Richter scale.

Moments slip pass as I'm getting myself together, the tension that has been vibrating through me for most of the afternoon slowly easing. I feel as if I can breathe again. My lungs not filling and drowning in the scent that is Knox.

I stand tall, looking at myself in the mirror and ignoring the flushed, hot mess that is my reflection looking back at me. Opening the large, mirrored unit I reach for the Advil, then close the mirrored door, jumping when I see Knox standing behind me. The air whooshes from my lungs, Knox snatching it from me as I gasp. I spin quickly, still clutching onto the pot of pills.

"Are you okay?" he steps closer to me and I feel the heaviness of his presence surround me.

"Yeah," I breathe, "just a headache," I shake the pills, willing for his eyes to break from mine and look at the pills. But it doesn't work.

"I'm real fucking mad at you," he reaches his hand forward, wrapping his fingers around the base of my throat.

"That's a shame," my eyes blaze with heat as I look up through my lashes at him.

"Are you going to keep taunting me with Jenkins?" His voice is thick as he keeps it low.

"Depends," I smirk, pulling my bottom lip in by my teeth.

"On?"

"If you're going to actually act as if I exist." I reach up, wrapping my fingers around his wrist and tug, but all that does is make him tighten his grip and I smile.

"You're fucking naughty."

"You've not seen anything yet," I taunt, leaning back against the sink and suddenly all willpower I had is ripped out of me.

"I can believe it," his hand reaches up my throat, until it reaches my chin, grabbing and running his thumb over my full bottom lip. I part my lips, drawing his thumb into my mouth and sucking.

"Little cub," he whispers, closing his eyes, his jaw clenching as he grinds his back teeth.

He pulls his thumb from my lips, his fingers flying to my jeans as he fumbles with the button and rips them from me.

"Naughty," I whisper, furrowing my brow. He smirks, stepping away as he twists the lock on the door.

His eyes fall to my white, lacy panties.

"Your cunt is already glistening," he rasps, his fingers rubbing through the material, rubbing my clit.

"I've been wet all day," I breathe, pushing my arms behind me and wrapping my fingers round the edge of the sink unit.

"Have you touched yourself?"

I shake my head, my breath trembling.

"Good," his arm snakes around my waist as he lifts me up, perching me on the space between the sinks. "Legs up," he orders and I do as he says, widening my legs for him, his eyes falling between them. Swirling his fingertips over my clit, his spare hand pulls my cropped tee up around my throat as he wraps his fingers there, holding me in position as well as my tee.

Lowering his lips around my hardened nipple, a low, vibrating moan courses through me.

"You need to keep quiet little cub, we don't want anyone to catch us now do we..." his fingers slip into the side of my panties, rubbing my clit before gliding his fingers through my parted pussy lips and plunging two fingers deep inside of me.

"Fuck," I whisper as his tongue laps over my nipple, sucking it into his mouth, his mouth hot.

His fingers slip out of me, before tugging on his sweat pants, kicking them down his legs.

"You clean?"

I nod, "Yeah, are you?"

"Haven't been with anyone in months, but yeah."

I feel a little shocked by his admission, but don't let him see it.

"I'm on the pill," I mumble.

"Wouldn't care if you wasn't. Once we fuck little cub, you're not going with anyone else," he strokes himself in long, slow strokes then pushes his thick tip at my tight opening. "You're mine from this moment on, do you understand me?" he rasps, his eyes levelling with mine and I nod.

"Yours."

My eyes roll in the back of my head as he slowly pushes his thick cock inside me, the burn caused by him stretching me taking my breath away.

"Tate." His grip around my throat tightens as he watches his cock slip in and out of me with ease. "Fuck, you feel so good. Your cunt is indescribable; so fucking tight." His jaw is tight, his teeth gritted as he fucks me slowly.

"Knox," I whisper moan, looking between us as his thick cock pulls to the tip, then slips straight back into me.

My heart races under my skin when I hear Cooper walk past the bathroom, muttering away to my dad. My eyes widen and Knox winks at me, smirking.

"Look at you getting fucked by me whilst your family are just outside the door," he moans, his thrusts speeding up. "You're such a naughty little girl, my little slut."

The degrading pet name slipping off his tongue brings my orgasm close. I clench down, my pussy tightening around him.

"You like that don't you? You like me degrading you like that?"

I nod, mewling as his voice floats through me, his cock hitting that spot.

"I think you can take more," he whispers, his head turning to the door then back to face me. "Do you?" he asks.

I nod eagerly, letting my eyes watch as his beautiful cock fucks me.

He smiles, looking down between us as he pulls his cock to his tip, then places two fingers at my opening, resting on top of his arousal coated cock.

Without warning, he pushes back into me, my mouth agape as my eyes roll in the back of my head.

"Fuck yes," I pant. Uncurling my white knuckled fingers from the edge, I reach between my legs and rub my swollen clit.

"You're so fucking greedy, I want your ass next," he grits, as he fucks me harder, my head hitting the mirrored unit.

My fingers rub faster, matching his thrusts into me.

"Are you okay Tate?" I hear my mum's voice, her fingers knocking on the door.

Knox grins at me, his eyes hooded as he slows his thrusts into me to a torturous pace, but still managing to fuck my brains out.

"Yeah!" I rush out, ignoring the urge to moan out after that.

"Okay darling."

Knox continues at the slow pace for a moment then picks up the pace again, fucking me hard.

"Fuck," I whisper, my eyes glassing as tears threaten, the pleasure ripping through me.

"Did Jenkins fuck you like this?" I see Knox's veins bulging and throbbing at his question and I shake my head. "Good, no one will fuck you like me." He grits, pulling his two fingers out then lowering them as he rubs my arousal around my tight ass. I don't have time to tense, his fingers are in me and they feel so fucking good.

My orgasm teeters as he pushes his cock deep into me, holding it there as he fingers my ass.

"I'm going to come," I whisper, tears rolling down my cheek at this overwhelming fullness that I feel. My pussy clamps down, I tilt my hips up so his long cock rubs on the spot I need.

"Come all over my cock, little cub. Coat me in your arousal," he whispers.

Pushing his thumb into my mouth, my eyes roll, my back arches and I come hard, my orgasm splintering me in two. I swear I see fucking stars, my ears ringing as the relief swarms me.

"Such a good fucking girl," he chokes, fucking me in short, hard thrusts, "I'm going to come," he whispers, filling my wet, greedy pussy full of his cum.

I pant, he pants, his face edging towards me as his lips cover mine.

"You're mine."

"Yours." I pant, breathless.

CHAPTER EIGHT
KNOX

Tate had been living with me for a year, and honestly, it had been the best year of my life. Sure, Mr and Mrs Alder weren't best pleased, but after a while they came round to the idea of me being head over heels in love with their daughter. Cooper struggled the most and ignored me for the best part of six months, but after a lot of pestering from me and letting him take his anger out on me on the ice, he calmed down.

Stepping out onto the ice, Cooper smiled as he hit me on the back.

"You ready for today?" he leans into me, his voice loud as excitement bubbles inside of him.

"I am buzzing," I beam at him before turning and seeing my ray of light hovering close to me and fuck does she look sexy in my jersey with my number on the back.

"Feeling confident are ya?" Cooper nudges into me, pulling my attention from Tate to him.

"So confident, we're going to smash these fuckers." I cheer and that was the truth. I was on a promise. Whilst riding me last night, Tate said that if we win I could handcuff her and fuck her sweet as fuck ass. There was no fucking way I was going to give that up.

"That's the spirit," Cooper grabs me, hugging me tightly before we start making our way onto the ice. Just before I step out, I turn to look at her one last time and she gives me a wink before blowing me a kiss. I reach my hand up, grabbing it and placing it on my heart.

Cheesy, but it was us.

It's what we done.

Grinning like the cat that was about to get the cream, I leaned over, handcuffing her delicate wrists to the bed, I skim my hand down her bare back before grabbing her hips and pulling her up onto her knees.

"You look so fucking pretty," I groan, rubbing my large hand over her bare ass cheek, giving it a gentle slap, then rubbing again before dipping my hand down her crease and plunging two fingers straight inside of her.

"Oh," she moans, pulling on the cuffs as pleasure ripples through her.

"Don't tug too hard baby, you'll mark your beautiful skin," I soothe, reaching forward and rubbing my thumb across the cool metal of the cuff.

"This is going to be quick, I have been hard since our win," I slip a third finger inside of her, stretching her and coating my fingers in her arousal.

"Knox," she breathes, her hips moving back as she grinds over my fingers.

"I know baby," I purr, pulling out of her and rubbing her arousal over her tight hole.

Fisting my hard cock, I rub my own arousal that is

sitting on my tip over her hole, pressing gently into her, stretching her. She tenses so I pull back, plunging my fingers inside her hot pussy again then gliding them between her cheeks and slipping them into her ass with ease.

"There we go, let's get you warmed up."

"Yes, baby, yes." I feel her moans vibrating through her core.

Pumping in and out of her, I fist myself once more before slipping my fingers from her, pressing the tip of my cock back at her opening and edging into her, bit by bit.

"Breathe baby, I promise this is going to feel so good," the restraint in my voice apparent as my eyes roll in the back of my head at how tight she is around me.

"Nearly there baby," I whisper, her hips gently rocking back and forth, easing me in. Stilling when she is full of me, I let her adjust before pulling out to the tip then slowly, gently, and only pushing half of me in, I fuck her slow.

"You feel so good little cub," I groan, my hands tightening round her hips as I lift a leg, bending at the knee as I fuck her at a better angle for both of us.

Curving one of my hands around her hip and slipping between her legs I rub and tease her clit.

"Fuck, Tate," I tip my head back and lose myself in the pleasure pool I am currently swimming in.

"Keep going," her voice is a whisper, begging me, "I need you to go harder."

I smile, letting my head fall forward as I watch my thick cock slip in and out of a hole that only I've been in.

"I can feel you getting so wet baby," I let her know, "your ass was made for me, you feel so fucking good," my thrusts getting harder into her.

"Yes, Knox, fuck, yes," she cries, her screams getting louder as I rub her clit and fuck her ass.

"That's it baby, let it go," I praise, "you're such a good girl, taking my cock so well baby."

"Knox," she whines, her voice shaky from my hard pounds into her.

"Come baby," I grit, tightening my grip on her hip, as my cock slips in and out of her ass with ease.

"Knox, yes. Yes!" She cries and I feel her whole body tighten and convulse as she comes, pulling on the handcuffs, her hips moving back and forth with me trying to get as much as she can from me. I slap her ass cheek hard as I come, roaring loud, my head tipping back as I spill into her.

After showering together, we lay arm in arm.

"I love you so much, Knox."

"Not as much as I love you baby."

She twists her upper body, my lips lower over hers as I kiss her, my tongue dancing with hers.

"You're my home, Tate."

ACKNOWLEDGMENTS

Dan. My best friend. My husband. My world. Thank you for pushing me to start this crazy journey. I love you to the moon and back.

Thanks firstly to Robyn, for keeping me in check and always being there when I needed you.

My girls, our little group. Thank you for the constant support and love you give me. I am so grateful to have you in my life and being with me on this crazy author journey.

My BETA's and friends, Sophie and Harriet. Thank you for being honest and loving my characters as much as I do.

Leanne, thank you for always being here for me. You're a friend for life.

Lea Joan, thank you once again for squeezing this in last minute. You have always been by my side in my author journey and I am so grateful that I get to work with you.

And lastly, my readers... without you, none of this would have been possible.
    My loyal fans, I owe it all to you.

Printed in Great Britain
by Amazon